Charlie's Story

MAEVE FRIEL

BEACON BOOKS

POOLBEG

For Paul, Aoife and Joe Kennedy

First published 1993 by
Poolbeg Press Ltd,
Knocksedan House,
123 Baldoyle Industrial Estate,
Dublin 13, Ireland

This edition published 1995

© Maeve Friel 1993

The moral right of the author has been asserted.

A catalogue record for this book is available from the British Library.

ISBN 1 85371 183 7

Cover illustrations by Alex Callaway
Cover design by Poolbeg Group Services Ltd
Set by Poolbeg Group Services Ltd in Stone 10/15
Printed by The Guernsey Press Ltd,
Vale, Guernsey, Channel Islands.

Praise for *Charlie's Story*

"Friel's language and dialogue are not unlike Anne Fine's: they are loaded with character implications."
Children's Books Ireland

Praise for *Distant Voices*

"Rarely in Irish children's writing has the time-slip theme been handled with such assurance."
Children's Books Ireland

"The general tone of displacement and unease suits the subject-matter and its environment, leaving the reader uneasy too."
The Irish Times

CONTENTS

CONTENTS

1

A TABOO IS BROKEN

Have you ever done the lottery? In our house every Saturday it was a ritual. Dad would come home from the early shift in the pub with a clutch of tickets. Then Noel and Vinnie, my uncles, and Peter, my dad, would sit around the table in Granny Bea's kitchen talking about how we'd spend the money if we won. Afterwards it was round to the sweet shop to put our numbers on the computer and into Paddy McCormack's for a pint (and a blackcurrant and lemonade for me, please, no ice). So to begin with, that Saturday started out the same as all the rest.

"There's one and a half million up for grabs tonight, I heard on the radio," Noel said, as he spooned coffee into the mugs and poured on boiling water.

Dad hung his coat on the back of a chair and dealt out the lottery papers, scattering them in four untidy piles in front of our chairs. "Two panels, Charlie," he said to me, "that's your lot, I'm not made of money."

"I know, I know," I said. "And I suppose you'll be looking for the money back, if my numbers win."

"You're not kidding. I'll be wanting a lot more than a quid."

For a couple of minutes there was silence in the kitchen as each of us gave serious thought to what we hoped would be the magical combination of birthdays, house numbers, bus routes and car registrations that would transform our lives, showering us with wealth and choices and opportunities.

"What would you do, Uncle Noel, if you won?" I said when I'd finished. I always asked him first—that was part of the ritual. Changing the order would wreck all our chances, just like coming up with a different way to spend the money every week was supposed to ward off bad luck. Our real dreams we kept hugged to ourselves.

Noel sucked in his cheeks. "If I got the big one? A farm, I think I might buy a farm."

Dad snorted with derision. "Jesus, Noel, you might as well take the money out to the far end of Dún Laoghaire pier and hurl it into the ocean."

"What do you mean? What's wrong with getting a farm?"

"I'll tell you what's wrong with it. You know nothing about animals. Stamp out hoose! Sure you don't know the meaning of the word. The closest brush you ever had with animal breeding was a dose of head lice." He picked up his coffee and winked at me.

"Ha, bloody ha," said Noel, offended. "We're talking gentleman farmer here. I wouldn't be the one walking about in pig-muck. It'd be an investment." He reached across the table and helped himself to one of my dad's cigarettes. (Noel is always giving up smoking so he only smokes other people's.) "I could have a ranch in South America. I wouldn't stay here anyway, not on your life."

Nobody spoke. Noel's bottom lip had turned inside out, the way it always did when he was in a huff. I knew it was my job to bring down the temperature again. I am a one-woman peace negotiator in this house. Don't get me wrong—it's not that they fight and argue and raise their voices. No, they do the exact opposite. Everybody clams up.

"What would you do, Dad?" I said, jogging him with my elbow. I could tell he had been waiting for this moment. He had probably been bursting to tell us his latest scheme since inspiration struck him. It usually did when he was pulling pints in the pub at lunch-time.

"Wait till you hear this, Charlie." His eyes were shining. "This is inspiration, with a capital I." He paused for a bit of dramatic effect, to make sure we were all paying attention. "Cable cars up to the top of Errigal!"

"You what?" Noel and I looked at one another, rolling our eyes. Errigal was a cone-shaped mountain in Donegal that we had all climbed one summer.

"It'll be the greatest tourist attraction in Ireland," Peter rushed on, "there's nothing like it in the entire country. We'd easily double our money. People would come from all over. I'd set up a whole string of cars coming from the far side of Dunlewy lake, and up the side of the mountain. We could have a sort of running commentary for the punters all about the local history, and then right up at the top a panoramic platform, 360 degrees, coffee and tea, telescopes... We'd double our money in no time."

I moved Dad's cup further in towards the middle of the kitchen table out of danger. He was waving his arms about, getting all worked up. As pipedreams went, this was a brand new one. I even liked the sound of it but you could see that Vinnie was not impressed—he drew in his breath loudly and pursed his lips. Perfectly formed rings of cigarette smoke floated slowly towards the ceiling. Dad looked at him uneasily.

"Weather," Vinnie said at last, moving his head from side to side in slow motion. "Have you thought how often it gets a wee bit cloudy and rainy up there in Donegal? Jesus, let's face it, you'd be closed more often than you'd be open."

"No way, they do it in Canada," Dad snapped back. "Myself and Lisa were up this mountain in the Rockies, gondolas they call cable cars there. We passed over the top of a bear, I swear. Lisa nearly went bananas."

Lisa. That was it. My mother's name. He didn't even notice

3

he'd said it. In more than ten years no one had ever mentioned my mother's name. I could scarcely breathe as the three men's voices chattered on in the background.

"One little snag there, Peter, old son," Noel was saying. "There are no bears in Donegal."

"No," agreed my dad. He drew heavily on his cigarette and knitted his eyebrows together. "Maybe we could put big polystyrene models of them, dotted here and there up the mountain sides."

"And a herd of plastic giant red Irish deer lapping at the side of the lake. Very realistic plastic." Noel hit the table with the side of his hand as the madness of the scheme seduced him. The three brothers clutched at each other, killing themselves laughing.

"Dad," I said, quietly. "That was my mum's name, wasn't it? Lisa?"

They turned to look at me with shocked, horrified expressions, their jaws hanging open. An ancient taboo had been broken. No one knew what to do. The three of them all reached simultaneously for the cigarette packet lying open in the middle of the lottery tickets and the dirty coffee cups.

2

COMING OUT OF THE TUNNEL

No one had ever said anything about what happened, neither Dad nor Granny Bea nor any of the uncles, but I could tell when they were thinking about it. There was just something about the way they looked at me and tilted their head to one side that I knew meant they were wondering, does she remember, does she remember anything at all?

Every year, especially around Christmas, I sensed the tension mount beneath the fevered preparations for the holidays. I saw the arched eyebrows and enquiring looks they exchanged among themselves if they came across me in a room by myself or looking a bit thoughtful. Everyone went out of their way to be kind, bringing me glasses of Coke when I was watching television and hinting mischievously about the presents I would be getting in the morning. Now and again one of the uncles would walk unsteadily into the sitting-room and give me a beery hug, saying something like, this will be the best Christmas ever, just you wait and see. What they didn't know and didn't dare ask was that I had remembered everything, everything but her name.

I remembered the roar of the train as it came rushing out of the tunnel and rattled to a stop at the platform. The woman, my mother, had pulled me along underground passages, past a man who was playing a guitar, and up the moving stairs—a long, long wooden staircase stretching as far as I could see. I stepped on to the creaking slats and stood to one side like the other people but mum wouldn't let the stairs do the work of carrying us up to the top. She jabbed my shoulder and pushed me up the stairs in front of her. I still remember the ache behind my knees, as my little legs climbed on and on and on, trying to avoid the parcels that banged against me.

It could have been outside a Body Shop that she left me. Even now sometimes when I'm walking past the branch in Grafton Street and smell that peculiar sweet fruity smell wafting out of the door, I can picture her thin white face leaning over me and saying, wait here a minute, Charlie, I have to make a phone call. My face must have crinkled up as if I might cry for she had put her face even closer to mine and said (in a very level, controlled voice that I knew spelt trouble), "Charlie, come on, Charlie, don't make a fuss." So I waited quietly, sitting on the little step outside the Body Shop, waiting for my mother to come back.

Can you believe that I was all but invisible to those millions of rushing people? A kid on her own in a big London railway station? It's incredible. (Now everywhere I go I have to keep my eyes peeled trying to spot lost children. I'm always swooping down on solitary wandering infants in supermarkets and chain stores.) I've no idea how long I sat there, in that London station, growing cold and hungry but knowing I must not make a fuss. "Don't fuss, Charlie," that's about the only thing I can remember my mother saying to me, "I can't cope if you fuss." So I never did.

All that afternoon only one woman, on her way out of the shop, stopped and asked me if I was lost. I remembered her suddenly looming up in front of me as she bent down. She had big green eyes, hair tied back in a springy pony-tail, and a face that seemed to be frowning and smiling at the same time.

"I'm waiting for my mum," I said, "she's in the phone box."

The woman scrunched up her eyes as if she might have been short-sighted and looked around the station, probably looking for the public telephone booths. Now when I think of her, I

6

suppose she had been concerned but it was Christmas Eve after all—no one wants to be drawn into someone else's hassles at a time like that. She probably had more shopping to do. I smiled to make her feel better. That's another thing my mother had trained me to do. "Smile, goddam you, Charlie. We don't want to look at your big sad face." The woman with green eyes had smiled back.

"If you're sure, then, sweetheart..."

Her voice had trailed off and she hurried away towards the trains, looking back once over her shoulder and giving me a guilty wave.

I don't know how much longer I was there. I remember the legs rushing past, legs in trousers, legs in boots, legs sticking out from under long coats, legs in short skirts, white legs, black legs. Bags banged against me but not one single goddam person said "excuse me." My bottom grew cold sitting on the cold step and I needed to have a pee. I pressed my legs tightly together and tried counting to one hundred like mum or one of her friends had taught me but it was too hard. I kept forgetting where I had got to, distracted by the travel announcements crackling over the loudspeaker and by the pushing, shoving crowds. In the end I stood up and skipped on one leg and then the other, jigging away to stop myself wetting my pants.

And then a policeman was bending down over me and saying, "Well, young lady, where's your mummy then?" and suddenly the shaming warm yellow pee was running down my legs and into my shoes.

Dad and Uncle Vinnie came to pick me up at the police station later that night.

"This is your dad," said the nice lady who had been with me. "He's going to take you back to his house for Christmas."

I didn't know who he was—I don't think I even knew what a 'dad' was.

The next morning we went on a plane and the air hostess

7

gave me a book to colour in and a model of an aeroplane that I still have on the window-ledge of my bedroom along with the Gary Gatwick teddy that Vinnie bought me. Dad and Vinnie drank little bottles of wine all the way over to Dublin and Dad said over and over, "Jesus, Vinnie, I can't believe that slag could leave a child of four years old just like that. I'll kill her if I ever clap eyes on her again."

"At least the cow put your phone number in the kid's pocket," Vinnie said.

At the airport in Dublin, there were photographers waiting for us when we came through customs. Vinnie lifted me up in his arms because Dad was carrying a bag of duty-free that clinked as he walked. When the reporters pressed forward, Vinnie pushed my head down on to his shoulders and shouted, leave the child alone, will you, and Dad thumped a cameraman who came too near. Then we went to Granny Bea's house where Christmas dinner was waiting. I had a huge family I knew nothing about—two more uncles, Noel and Chris, as well as Dad and Vinnie and Granny Bea.

I was very quiet, frightened, I suppose, by all the strange people and the funny way they talked. Dad had to cut up my meat in small pieces. He showed me how to hold a knife and fork and tucked a big red napkin under my chin. Before then, with Lisa, I had mostly eaten bags of chips and fruit and stuff that didn't have to be cooked. The whole family sat around the table, watching me.

Afterwards, I fell asleep still sitting at the table. Someone carried me upstairs to bed and even though I didn't want to be on my own in the big unfamiliar bedroom, I didn't cry and didn't make a fuss. Everybody stood around the end of the bed looking at me and saying I was a great kid and a real little looker into the bargain and Granny Bea said wasn't it a mercy that nothing worse had happened, considering some of the weirdos that you get in London.

So I stayed on, growing up in the big house near Dún Laoghaire, pretending like the rest of them that nothing odd had ever happened, that I had always been there. I suppose my life was normal after that—I went to school and learned to ride a bike and swim and do a back-somersault. Uncle Chris went to live in Boston but Vinnie and Noel and Dad still live here. Dad's a barman now though he used to change jobs nearly as often as I changed class. He's been a painter and a driver and a postman. Last summer he had a sort of oven on wheels and sold baked potatoes outside pubs until someone threatened to report him for food poisoning. (Though Dad said it was hardly his fault: the potato was the least of the man's problems after the amount of jar he'd had.) Every so often, Granny Bea tells him he should have finished his exams and made something of himself, he was wasting a good brain.

I sometimes have flash-backs about the London thing, like when I walk past the Body Shop, or sometimes when I hear Christmas carols. Once, a year or so ago, I was watching a documentary about homeless people in London and they showed a tube station and one of those big wooden escalators. My stomach turned over. I was all by myself in the house except for Granny who was in the kitchen ironing. I went out to talk to her about it—my mouth was so dry I didn't even know that I was going to be able to speak—I could feel my throat tightening — but when I saw her at the ironing-board, a strand of her grey-blonde hair falling over her face, she looked too fragile, too easily wounded, I didn't like to make a fuss.

So until last summer when dad slipped it out about seeing the bear in Canada, no one had ever mentioned my mother's name in more than ten years or spoken about how I came to be here. Little did I think that soon everyone would find out that I was the Abandoned Baby.

3

STICKS AND STONES

They were still behind me, and getting closer. I didn't have the nerve to turn around to face them head-on but I wouldn't give them the satisfaction of seeing me break into a run. If I did that they would come out from the shop-doorways or from behind the parked cars, wherever it was they were hiding, whooping and jeering at me. I couldn't stand them swarming all around me like hateful malevolent wasps, not yet anyway. That would come later. No, it was best to pretend it was just a game, even if I had to let them win.

The footsteps following behind me sounded closer. Was it just my imagination or were the whispering voices talking about me, teasing and mocking, laughing at the way I walked, at my hair, mimicking my voice? No, it was not my imagination. I recognised Lorna's sneering voice and Tara and Natalie giggling like the boot-lickers they were. They were taking up from where they had left off on the last day of term before Christmas. Nothing had changed.

I pulled up my gabardine collar against the sleet and began to walk faster. The school gates were still about five minutes' walk away. In the distance I could see the giant yellow crane looming over the site where they were building the new classrooms and science block. A bus braked noisily and came on to the roundabout a couple of hundred yards in front of me: I'll show them, I thought. I continued walking on at the same pace, timing myself so that I would come level with the bus just as it reached the stop on the other side. Before they could suspect anything, I'd rush across the road and get on it, even though it was going the wrong direction, taking me further away from the school. Grimly, I walked on, keeping my eyes fixed on the approaching bus. With any luck, I would catch them completely off-guard—they wouldn't have time to follow me. And who cared if I was late for assembly—at least round one, day one, would be mine. There was no way I was putting up with another term like the last one.

There were two women standing at the stop already, the younger one sheltering behind the advertising hoarding, her back turned against the biting wind. The other one walked forward to the kerb and put out her arm to flag down the bus. It began to slow and pull in. Without bothering to check the traffic, I stepped out on to the road and dashed straight into the path of a bread delivery van. It skeetered dangerously out of my way into the middle of the road and the oncoming traffic. A car screeched to a halt, horn blaring. All of a sudden an arm yanked me back to the pavement. Dazed and shaken, I swung around. A boy in a parka jacket, still holding on to the strap of my school-bag, was grinning at me.

"Don't do it," he said. "Too messy, too much blood."

I stared at him for an instant, wondering what he was talking about, then shook him off.

The girls who had been following me rushed forward, yelling. As I had guessed it was Lorna and her cronies.

"Jesus, Snotty Lottie's doing a kamikaze stunt!"

"Can't hack it any more, eh, Charlotte, going to do yourself in?"

On the other side of the road, the doors of the bus closed and the orange indicator light blinked as the driver began to pull out. It was now or never. I took a chance, darted out into the middle of the road and banged on the side of the bus to attract the driver's attention.

"Hey, open up, will you?"

"Jesus, are you trying to kill yourself or what?" said the driver scathingly.

I stumbled up the steps of the bus, my heart thumping. The inside of my mouth tasted like chalk.

"The next stop please."

"You mean you nearly caused a pile-up to go one stop?" The driver gave me a filthy look as I put down my money. I just shrugged.

Across the road, Lorna and the others gaped as I walked down the aisle of the bus. One of them waved sarcastically, the others gestured obscenely. The boy who had pulled me back from the edge had walked on. I hadn't even thanked him.

✳✳✳

The bell had already gone when I arrived at the school. I sneaked through the side gate even though it was out of bounds since the builders came on site and ran past the library. Everyone was already in the hall at assembly. Standing on tiptoes, I peered through the high glazed section of the hall door. The head was on the platform, welcoming everyone back after the Christmas break. She hoped everyone would have a very happy and successful New Year. Some chance, I thought. I ducked down quickly before anyone spotted my face at the glass. If I hung around without being spotted until the end of assembly I could fall in with the crowds as they came out and headed for their form rooms.

"What are you doing here, Charlotte? Arriving late on the very first day of term doesn't augur well for the rest of the year."

(Augur well, I ask you—but that's the way people talk around here.)

12

The deputy head, Mrs Armstrong, had appeared from nowhere, bearing down on me from the other end of the corridor, her black gown flapping importantly behind her.

"I'm afraid that's a detention mark, first day or not. It's not a promising start to the new year, is it? No," she continued, putting a finger to her lips when I started to protest, "you know the rules. Now follow me."

In despair, I followed Mrs Armstrong down the seemingly interminable centre aisle to the front of the hall, while five hundred smug heads swivelled around to watch me. The head had stopped in mid-sentence and watched, tight-lipped, until I fell into line beside the rest of my class. Singled out again, on the very first day, I was thinking. I was wondering if I looked as red as I felt. Behind me I heard a little explosion of laughter and a familiar voice whispered, wouldn't you just know it, it's the Abandoned Baby.

❋❋❋

The first day of a new term is always weird, as if everyone has to grow back into their school skins again, skins that no longer fitted as well as they had done just a few weeks previously. Teachers, flushed and battered by the effects of too many late nights and hangovers, rushed headlong down corridors. They ordered people about as if that would somehow make their own guilt and sense of loss disappear. (I know the syndrome: my dad and Vinnie and Noel do exactly the same thing.) Others, refreshed and tanned from skiing trips or apartment holidays in the Canary Islands, stopped to talk to their favourites, accepting compliments on their tans, asking after their mothers and fathers.

Things had changed in my class too—girls who before the holidays had been mouse-like and shy had sprouted breasts, or, at the very least, had got new bras, and sat on the edge of their desks, shoulders back, waist sucked in, to show off their new improved profiles. Some had got off with boys at Christmas parties and huddled at the back of the form-room, giggling and shrieking with laughter as they recounted their exploits to anyone who would listen.

I went into the room very quietly and walked straight over to the wall of grey lockers at the side of the room to unload my books and sports kit. One or two girls nodded half-heartedly at me but most ignored me. They had all learnt that siding with Charlie just wasn't worth it. I almost preferred it that way. There had been times during the first term when I thought someone was my friend, only to be deserted or betrayed when I least expected it. It was as if Lorna and Tara and Natalie had the power to poison everyone against me. They were forever creating circles, cliques, which on whim they would open up to include new members.

"Do you want to play tennis doubles with us after school?" they might say to someone out of the blue. Or they invited other girls home to tea. No one ever refused. Everyone wanted to be friends with rich, good-looking, clever Lorna.

At other times they pulled their circle tightly closed against all the others. At those times they spoke only to each other, and then only in some private coded language they had invented.

"Wheggy deggideggy Cheggarleggie's meggothegger abeggandeggon hegger?"

I think they thought they were God's chosen people or something. It would make you laugh, if they weren't so treacherous. Some day I knew they would go too far.

In all their games, in all the shifting sands of the alliances they created and destroyed, there was only one rule: I was untouchable. I was always outside the circle. I was beyond the pale.

It was Lorna who found out about my being dumped in London by my mother. Lorna's father is something in television.

Every morning for the first few weeks after the summer holidays, he dropped Lorna off at the school gates in a large shiny car with black windows. Sometimes Tara and Natalie had a lift too. They would all slide out of the car, shouting in too-loud voices like spoilt brats, blowing kisses to Lorna's father and waving goodbye until he drove off, with a jaunty toot-toot on his horn.

One morning in October, I was walking to school. The rain was sheeting down, huge raindrops rebounding off the pavement up to my thighs. I had my head down, almost buried in my chest, so I didn't notice the car until it had stopped right beside me. A rear window slid down, noiselessly, and a voice said, can we offer you a lift?

I had hardly spoken to Lorna before then. She was in my class, of course, but most of her set were the girls who had come up from the junior school—people who had transferred from other national schools just didn't count. The car was the most comfortable I had ever been in with deep squidgy leather seats— and also the most powerful. It was like travelling on the back of a strolling tiger. I could hardly wait to tell Dad.

"What's your name, young lady?" Mr Higgins asked, studying me in his rear-view mirror.

"Charlotte Collins," I said, horrified to see that my hair was plastered against my head in dripping rat's tails and that, in the heat of the car, steam was rising off my coat. Something about him made me feel poor and awkward. I began to feel sorry I had accepted the lift.

"That rings a bell," he said. "Do I know your folks? What's your dad's name?"

"Peter Collins."

He repeated the name as if he thought he recognised it. "Rugby club man, is he?"

I said he preferred soccer actually.

"Peter Collins. Charlotte. There's something I just can't put my finger on."

He adjusted the angle of the rear-view mirror again and looked back at me, narrowing his eyes. I gave him a very embarrassed smile. By the time we stopped at the school gates I was desperate to get away. I started to open the door but Lorna's father swivelled around in the driver's seat and looked at me straight in the face, holding my gaze until it became really unnerving. Then he smiled, a big open smile that transformed his face, and snapped his fingers.

"Got it," he said. He was very good-looking, like Lorna.

"Got what?" asked Lorna.

"Never mind, sweetheart. Tell you later. Work hard."

With that he moved off with his usual toot-toot.

All day, Lorna had me sit beside her. At break, we sat on the bench beside the tennis court while she told me about her holidays in Montpellier in France. At lunch-time, she gave me a packet of smoky bacon crisps in exchange for my mini Mars bar. During French, she chose me as her partner for the paired work. After the last bell, she said I could be her best friend. I was so happy I went home and drew two intertwined hearts on my homework diary, the initials CC and LH locked together at their centre in a flourish of red felt pen. It's hard to believe I did that now.

I went to school the next morning in a fever of anticipation. Even when the shiny black car passed me by without offering me a lift, I didn't suspect a thing. I rushed down the corridor listening to the din coming from the form-room and wondering what was up. But the moment I entered, the room fell silent. People moved shiftily to their desks or lockers as if caught in the act of some shameful crime. No one spoke to me. If I spoke to anyone, they turned their back on me. If I sat near anyone, they froze me out. When I sat down beside Lorna at lunch, she picked up her plate and went to another table. At gym, I couldn't find anyone to be my partner. At playtime, girls huddled in small whispering groups until I approached when they fled shrieking with shrill voices. What was it all about? What had I done? Even then, I remember thinking it must be my fault.

At four o' clock, I hung around the cloakroom until everyone but Monica Hamilton had left. Monica was large and soft and spotty and the thickest girl in our class. People would die of embarrassment if they had to sit beside her or were paired up with her—and Monica knew it. If she had a clue why I was getting the cold shoulder, she'd tell me. She'd know how I was feeling.

Monica saw me the moment she shuffled out of the cubicle and slunk embarrassed to the hand-drier, her eyes cast down.

"What's going on, Monica?"

She punched the hot air drier again and kept her back turned from me. Her broad soft shoulders rose and fell in a slow-motion shrug.

"Come on, Monica, tell me. It's not fair," I said, moving closer and putting my hand on her shoulder.

She jerked my hand off and turned to face me, her big cratered face bright with embarrassment. Beads of sweat had broken out on her upper lip. Did she think I was going to beat her up?

"They say you have bad blood," she stammered. "They say we're not to talk to you."

"What are you talking about?" I think I laughed. I couldn't imagine what she meant. "Who said it?"

"Lorna said your mother walked out on you when you were a baby. She said you were so screwed-up even your mother couldn't stand you. She said all your family are wasters."

For a moment, I couldn't breathe.

"How can they know about that?" I thought. "Only I know what happened. And I've never talked about it to anyone."

It was as if I had been punched really hard in the pit of my stomach and completely winded. Blood rushed to my face. I could feel the sting of tears behind my eyes. I swallowed hard and tried to speak but my mouth just opened and closed uselessly. Monica saw her chance and rushed towards the door. Before she left, she turned around triumphantly and sneered, "And she said you're a bastard."

I don't think I had ever felt afraid before that afternoon but I stood in that cloakroom and felt my skin grow clammy and my chest tighten with fear. It was as if I knew what was going to happen, that, from that day on, my life at school would be hell.

"Keep a low profile," Uncle Vinnie advised me, "if they start to annoy you. Ignore them." But, of course, Vinnie didn't know the half of it. I had started to tell him that I didn't want to go back to school when he walked into the kitchen on New Year's Eve and found me in bits. Vinnie meant well but he probably didn't even remember talking to me the next day for he had been pretty well tanked up. Myself and Granny Bea were the only two sober people in the house for most of the Christmas holidays—but you couldn't tell Granny anything. Sticks and stones may break my bones, she had said once, but words will never hurt me. What did she know? Had anyone ever called her, Charlotte the harlot? or Snotty Lottie or, worst of all, the Abandoned Baby? The one thing that nobody had ever talked about.

The main problem with Granny was that she shut out anything unpleasant from her life. Bad smells, bad vibes, badness. It was as if she thought these things didn't exist provided she refused to notice them. Dad was useless too. It must be in their genes, this inability to face facts. The one time I had ever said anything to him about hating school and how horrible everyone was, you know what he said?

"Don't provoke them, Charlie, maybe it's something you do that gets on their nerves. Try to get on with them."

So much for parental support.

Every night I looked at myself in the long mirror in the bathroom. My face had become pointy and thin, my eyes sunk in deep hollows. I smoothed the skin above my cheek-bones, trying to rub away the bruised purple shadows below my eyes. I didn't dare stand on the scales in the bathroom for I knew I was losing weight. Alone among all the girls in my class, I had no chest. I was completely flat. My skirt hung on bony hips, taking on a life of its own, sliding around so that I would sometimes find the back at the front. No wonder people hated me. I looked ugly and poor and a loser.

I had started to pull my hair out of my head, deliberately tugging at little clumps of it so that here and there I had little bald patches. If you looked closely, you could see scabs on my skull where the hair and skin had been yanked out. My nails too were disgusting but I gnawed at them, anyway, pulling at the cuticles and the flesh around them until the blood flowed. Even that didn't stop me. I would beaver away at any loose strips of skin, chewing away regardless of the pain.

✳✳✳

"All right, class, settle down."

Miss Morrison, the form mistress, appeared at the door and cast her usual cold unsmiling look around the classroom. "Everyone sit down, please. We've a lot of work to get on with."

"Welcome back, miss," piped up Lorna, at her most simperish, from the back row, "and a Happy New Year."

My lip curled at Lorna's two-facedness and I was delighted when Miss Morrison ignored her. Instead she briskly walked to her table at the front of the room and stared coldly at the chattering sex machines at the back of the class until they reluctantly moved forward and sat at their desks. Without a word of welcome or any reference to the Christmas holidays, she began to call the register. My mood just plummeted. Why did everybody in the whole school behave so horribly all the time? It was as if there was a curse on the place; bad humour and small-mindedness oozed from every wall and seeped up from under the floor-boards so that everyone became infected.

I held out my fingers to examine them, loathing myself for hurting myself like this, even as I put my fingers back in my mouth to mutilate the nail itself, gouging it out from the living flesh beneath.

"Charlotte, stop day-dreaming or giving yourself a manicure, whatever you're up to. Make yourself useful and hand around the work-books." A pile of maths books landed with a thump on my desk.

"Some manicure!" I thought as I walked up and down the aisles, distributing the books. "Ten out of ten for observation, Miss Morrison."

Tara and Lorna were sitting next to one another, about four rows back from the teacher's desk. Just as I placed Tara's workbook on her desk, she picked it up between her finger and thumb as if I had just put something repulsive, something utterly corrupt and stinking in front of her, and ostentatiously rubbed it on the sleeve of her jumper.

"Charlotte's germs," she groaned in a loud sotto voce whisper and grimaced at Lorna. Lorna sniggered and she too rubbed her work-book with the back of her sleeve.

"Charlotte's germs," she repeated to Natalie in the row behind. A low titter of laughter rippled through the classroom as the phrase was passed around. I seethed with anger.

"Charlie, stop messing about," snapped old Morrison. "We haven't got all day."

Lorna smirked. As I turned away, her side-kick Tara stretched her leg out in front of me. I half stumbled but managed to stop myself falling over by grabbing at the desk in front. The workbooks that I was carrying scattered in an untidy heap across the floor. As I stooped to pick them up, a low infectious ripple of laughter ran around the room.

"Charlotte, I won't warn you again," thundered Morrison. "You're far too old for that sort of playing to the gallery. I believe

20

you've already got one detention mark today for being late—I won't hesitate to give you another. Now pass around the rest of those books and and stop acting the clown. The holidays are over."

I went back to my seat, smarting with the injustice of it. I stared sullenly ahead, seeing in my mind's eye the days stretching into weeks, the weeks into months, the months into years before I could break free of these sick people, leave the whole hateful lot of them behind.

4

TALKING TO CASSO

I was at the bus-stop after school when the boy in the parka came along and sat on the low wall behind the shelter. He was carrying his school books in a plastic bag which he threw down at his feet. After a while he began to rummage in his pockets, pulled out the butt of a cigarette and lit up. After no more than a couple of drags, he seized up with a coughing fit and tossed the fag out into the middle of the road, creating an arc of red ash. I watched him from behind the advertisement on the bus shelter, wondering if I should speak to him. For a minute or two he was absolutely still, staring into nowhere. Then suddenly, he stood up and moved out to the edge of the kerb, looking down the road to see if a bus was coming. There was not. He stamped his feet and plunged his hands deeper into the pockets of his thin coat. He was standing so close to me I could have reached out and touched his face.

"You're not going to throw yourself under another bus, are you?" He turned around suddenly and grinned at me. "My reactions mightn't be as fast the second time."

"It wasn't deliberate," I sort of stammered. He must have known I was there all the time, watching me watching him.

"What were you running away from anyway?"

"Oh nothing. I had to go back home for something."

He raised an eyebrow. "Didn't look like that to me. Looked

like those girls were giving you a hard time."

I didn't answer. I hate talking at bus stops. There are always too many other people standing there, with nothing better to do than listen to other people's conversation. After a moment, he walked forward to the roadside again to check if the bus was coming and stayed there, at the kerb.

When the bus came a few minutes later, there was a great surge forward as everyone tried to get on first—as if this was the last bus on the planet. When I eventually managed to get through the scrum and looked around for a seat, there was only one place, down at the back of the bus, beside the boy.

I gave him a sort of half-smile but he ignored me and looked out the window. He was a good bit older than me, I reckoned, about sixteen, and not good-looking exactly but okay. He wasn't wearing a school uniform, just jeans and docs and a green parka, and he had one earring. The tips of his fingers were stained brown from smoking the butts of cigarettes.

"Got me figured out yet?" He turned to face me and gave me another of his grins. I saw my face drop in the reflection of the bus in the dark road outside—of course, he had been watching me, watching him.

"What's your name, anyway?"

"Charlie," I said.

"Hi ya, Charlie." He put out his hand to shake mine, but not in a mock adult way. He was dead serious. "I'm Casso and I'm getting off here. Take care. Remember what your mother taught you—look right and left and right again before you cross the road." He tapped the back of my shoulder as he squeezed past. I watched him move through the crush of people standing in the aisle of the bus until he disappeared from view in the throng around the door.

As the bus pulled away from the stop, I saw him again, striding down the road with long loping steps towards the flats. He looked invulnerable, whereas I, gnawing at my bleeding fingers, felt as if I was flaking away, like some old fragile laboratory specimen, turning into dust.

✳✳✳

Dad was on the phone when I came into the hall. The light was off and the sound of the television blared from the open door of the sitting-room. He must have rushed out to answer the phone without stopping to switch on the hall light. As I passed, he cupped the receiver in his hand and muttered something in a low voice. I threw my bag into the cupboard under the stairs and walked through to the kitchen.

"I suppose I'll still recognise you?" I heard him saying with a funny sort of embarrassed laugh.

A couple of minutes later, I heard the ping of the telephone as he hung up.

He followed me into the kitchen, folding a little yellow sheet of paper and tucking it away in his wallet.

"That was Paddy from the pub," he said. "I've got to change shifts. Tell Ma I won't be home till late."

I could see he was trying to avoid looking at me. The lie hung between us, making us both too embarrassed to say anything. He opened the door of the fridge and broke off a piece of cheese.

"I'll be off then, Charlie. Don't forget to tell Ma."

The front door banged, sending a draught through the house that rattled the window-panes and made something fall to the floor in an upstairs bedroom.

I walked out to the hall table and examined the note pad we keep there for messages. The top page was empty but he had pressed so hard on the page that he had torn off that you could still make out one word.

L.I.S.A. it said, in sloping capital letters, and another word, crossed out.

My stomach churned. Had she telephoned our house? Was

he going to see her? Was she back in Ireland? Was she going to take me away?

The Abandoned Baby, I thought bitterly. How could my dad even speak to her?

5

CHARLIE ON THE RAILS

Some days were normal, if normal meant nothing really horrible happened—no one stole my lunch money or beat me up or got me into trouble with one of the teachers—but the war went on. I might hear Lorna and her friends laughing at the way I chewed or they might all screw up their noses when I walked into the room and say, isn't there a funny smell in here all of a sudden. I had to be forever on my guard, eyes and ears on full alert. The worst part was always having to pretend I didn't care. I never cried, I never grassed. "Don't make a fuss, Charlie," that was what Lisa had drummed into me, even on the day she walked away from me. I had learned that lesson well.

So that it would never let me down by releasing hateful smells, I scrubbed my body every evening until the skin peeled back, exposing raw flesh. Feet, armpits, teeth, private places, there seemed no end to the treacheries of the body ... Personal hygiene became my obsession. I carried a deodorant in my school-bag and scuttled in and out of the cloak-room to re-apply it several times a day.

Changing the way I chewed was harder. I practised in front of the triple mirror in Granny's bedroom. Sitting on the low stool, watching my three faces, one before me, one to the left of me, one to the right of me, three mouths clamped shut, jaws working, the muscles of my face miming breaking down the crusts of tuna fish sandwiches. I couldn't see what I was doing wrong. It didn't look any different to the way anyone else did it. In the end, I stopped eating at school, it was the easiest thing to do. Soon I was eating practically nothing, at least not in public.

Winter had settled on the city like a shroud. Wet clammy mists blew in off the sea during the night. I walked to school in the dark and came home in the dark, trudging along wet roads, yellow street lights reflected in dark oil-streaked puddles. Water dripped from bare trees, piles of dirty leaves lay up against walls where they had drifted after the last autumn storms. The toothy faces of politicians stared down on the streets from rain-streaked election posters. I wondered what crime I had committed in another life that I had to come back and live this hell.

"Hi, Charlie," the voice behind me said. It was Tara, Lorna's best friend.

The hairs stood up on the back of my neck—what did she want? Why was she behaving as if we were friends?

I said nothing.

"Come on, Charlie, don't be like that. I just wanted to walk beside you. There's no harm in that, is there?"

I shrugged but kept moving quickly. I didn't know if there was any harm in it or not. I had learnt to trust no one.

"I'm sorry Lorna is so mean to you. We know it's not your fault your mother abandoned you. I think it was really cruel of her."

Tara moved nearer to me and stuck her arm through mine. I pulled my arm away, as if I had just had an electric shock, and spun around to see if there was anyone watching us. If this was some sort of practical joke, I didn't want to be taken in.

"Come on, Charlie," Tara lisped in a cute babyish voice, trying to make me smile. "Don't be like that. I really like you. Lorna Higgins is just a stupid snob."

She walked beside me all the way to the school. I tried to trail behind a little, and didn't speak. It was probably some sort of a dare that Lorna had put her up to, I decided. Afterwards Tara would have to report back what I had said, if I had been taken in by her offer of friendship, if I had done anything they could use against me later.

Tara stuck by me like a barnacle on a rock at the seaside. She followed me into the cloakroom where we hung up our coats. I went to the loo to throw her off but when I came out again, she was still there, calmly going through the pockets of all the coats.

"Tara, what are you doing?" I said.

She shrugged. "Nothing, hardly anyone had any money, anyway," she said, pocketing a handful of small change.

"It's not fair, Tara," I began but she brushed me aside.

"Don't be so wet, Charlie. It's only a few pence."

Outside there was the sound of adult heels clicking down the wooden floor of the corridor. I froze, guiltily, even though I hadn't done a thing.

"Christ," said Tara, "old Strongarm on her morning rounds. I'm out of here." She bolted into one of the cubicles down at the end of the room but didn't lock the door.

As I ran out of the cloakroom into the corridor, I walked straight into the chest of Mrs Armstrong. I leaped back in fright and raced towards my classroom, heart pounding. I knew that would not be the end of it.

During the last lesson before break, Tara jumped to her feet, with a theatrical shriek and asked to be excused. She had left her watch in her coat pocket, she said, her granny's gold watch. Could she go to the cloakroom and get it? Needless to say, when she came back a few minutes later, throwing the door open wide, tears were streaming down her face. The watch had been stolen.

I suppose the teacher told everyone in the staffroom at break-time what had happened. Then Mrs Armstrong would have remembered seeing me running scared out of the cloakroom earlier that morning. All they had to do then was jump to conclusions. Mrs Armstrong hated me anyway.

"Will Class 3C please return immediately to their form-room?" The announcement boomed out over the PA system. We trailed back, expecting trouble.

One by one we had to turn out our pockets on to our desks. Then we stood around the sides of the rooms, silent and cowed as the two teachers moved from desk to desk, searching our belongings. The watch was found hidden among the papers in my drawer.

"I didn't take it, I didn't," I blurted out as Mrs Armstrong triumphantly held up a gold wrist-watch. The class gasped. All heads turned to look at me.

"Tara, tell them," I pleaded, hating the pathetic sound of my own voice, feeling myself grow bright red. "I didn't touch your watch."

Tara looked at me, sadly, with her tear-stained face. "Oh Charlotte," she said, "how could you do this to me when I was trying to be your friend?"

I ran towards her and began to thump her with my fists. "You were not. You set this up."

Mrs Armstrong dragged me off her and held my arms tightly back behind my back.

"You come with me, young lady," she said coldly and pushed me towards the door. As it closed behind us, a clamour of voices started up. Above the din I heard Lorna say, "Poor Tara, are you all right?"

Neither the head nor the deputy seemed interested in hearing my side of the story. They rang my dad but he obviously said he couldn't come around to the school—his shift at the pub started at twelve o'clock. He would drop in on his way home for his break at five.

"I must insist you come, Mr Collins," said the head, scowling at me. "Charlotte has not only stolen a watch but has also assaulted the girl who owned it. I'm afraid I have no option but to suspend her for a week."

Dad must have been a bit abusive for she made a sharp intake of breath, and held the receiver out from her face as if it had given her an electric shock. Good old Dad, I thought, at least he knows I'm not a thief.

For the rest of the day, I had to sit in a corner of the secretary's office, working by myself. What did they think I might do—infect the rest of my class with my bad attitude? Every visitor to the school office, from the man to fix the photocopier to the foreman of the building site who came in to use the phone, they all felt obliged to look at me and make some comment—Not feeling well? In the doghouse?—And the secretary would break off whatever she was doing and say, really disapprovingly, as if she was the one in charge of the stinking school, "Actually, Charlotte is in very serious trouble." When the bell went at four o'clock, the head swept in and told me to go home. She gave me a list of homework for every subject and strict instructions for my dad to get in touch immediately.

Outside, groups of girls were hanging around the school gates. I couldn't face them. Ignoring the DANGER, KEEP OUT sign, and the angry warning shouts of a man driving a fork-lift truck laden with wooden pallets of bricks, I cut through the building site. A deep rectangular pit had been gouged out of the earth where the foundations of the new classrooms would be laid. I ran past it and emerged through a gap in the fence near the railway station.

It was then that I saw them. A flash of blue blazer disappearing behind the metal railway bridge told me all I needed to know. They were waiting for me, waiting to ambush me. I walked more slowly, wondering how many there were, torn between standing up to them and flying off in the opposite direction, but before I had decided, a head ducked out again from behind the railings. This time, they spotted me and with a great whoop, three of them came running forwards, jeering and shouting at me.

"Snotty Lottie's gone and got herself suspended!"

"The Abandoned Baby's nothing but a thief!"

"Little bastard thought she could get away with it."

I stood my ground. Lorna, Tara and Natalie closed in around me, locking me inside their malicious circle, poking and jabbing at me.

"Why did you set me up like that, Tara?" I said. "I never touched your stupid watch—you were the one who was picking people's pockets."

"Oh, I never did, you liar." Tara leaned forward to pull my hair but I moved back. Her hand caught the strap of my schoolbag and it slid off my shoulder on to the ground. Lorna picked it up and ran off a short way, dangling the bag at arm's length, daring me to come and take it from her.

"You want it? Come and get it."

I lurched forward to catch the bag but she raised it higher, teasing me, swinging it above her head until it was spinning in ever faster circles. I leapt at it, trying to seize it as it came past me, but it was no use. I kicked out at Lorna, catching her full on the shin. She cried out and let go of the strap. The bag sailed over our heads, falling over the iron bridge railings and down on to the tracks below where it landed with a solid thump.

All four of us ran to the railings and looked over. The bag lay between the sleepers of the railway line on the far side. Tara gave a nervous giggle.

"Well," said Lorna, looking at me with her commanding blue eyes, "you'll have to go down and get it. You could cause an accident. You could be fined for obstructing the line."

The three faces moved closer to mine, daring me to climb down onto the electric line. I could taste the blood in my mouth from biting the insides of my cheek.

"You'd better do it, Charlie. Before your bag derails a train. Could you live with all those deaths on your hands?"

"Go away," I screamed, "leave me alone."

For a fraction of a second, Lorna's cold busybody expression faltered. For once she looked doubtful, as if she thought she might have gone too far.

"It's your own fault," she began, "you shouldn't have called Tara a pick-pocket..."

"Go away," I shouted again.

I sat down on the edge of the pavement and put my hands over my ears so I didn't have to listen to them any more. After a while when I realised they had gone, I stood up and looked down onto the railway tracks. I hadn't heard a DART pass by for some time so I needed to act quickly. I hauled myself over the handrail of the the bridge and gingerly let myself drop on to the nearside of the embankment. The bank fell away steeply to the tracks.

I slithered down through the clumps of wet fern and muddy grass, clutching at rocks and brambles which caught and tore at my coat and stockings. My bag lay only a few yards away on the far track, the side the trains used coming out from the city centre, but those few yards seemed like infinity to me. I picked myself up and edged cautiously towards the near rail. Was it really live? Would I get a shock if I touched it? Why had I never asked anyone about this before? I stepped into the middle of the track, trembling and half-blinded with tears.

Suddenly there was a loud roar and a train came bearing down on me, on the nearside. I stumbled back up the embankment, grabbing at clumps of grass, anything I could grip on to, but they all came away in my hand. The siren blared in my ears as the train shot noisily past me. Caught in the glare of the brightly-lit carriages, I froze, skewered, spotlit like an escaper from a prisoner of war camp.

Warily, I dropped down beside the track again and looked up and down. The draught caused by the passing train had caught my bag and tossed it a few feet further away. It lay up against the far rail, its long strap hanging across the sleeper. I stepped forward, preparing to make a dash for it, when suddenly, another train came hurtling towards me from the other direction. I scrambled back up the bank as fast as I could, trying to block out the sound of the derailment that was almost sure to happen. I grabbed out at the handrail of the bridge, but was so scared I didn't have the energy to haul myself over. I gripped the frozen metal with white knuckles, listening to my breath coming in short painful gasps, and the machine-gun rattle of the train as it disappeared down the track to Dalkey.

When at last I had the courage to turn around and look down, my bag had been carried off, its contents scattered to the four winds. I pulled myself over the bridge and walked, empty-handed, down the hill towards home, all hope of rescuing my belongings abandoned.

"Jesus, Charlie!" were the first words that greeted me when I walked in the front door. "What have you been doing to yourself?"

Dad was standing at the hall table, the phone in his hand as if he was about to make a call or had just finished. He replaced the receiver and stared at me, horrified.

I looked down. My coat and shoes were caked with muck, a trickle of blood was oozing down one of my legs and there was a ragged tear running down one sleeve of my gabardine. My face and hair probably looked a sight too.

"I fell," I said.

"Jesus, Charlie, you're running wild." His voice was hard and cold. "What's all this about stealing a watch too? That battle-axe of a head teacher of yours was on to me this morning, giving me a load of grief about you. I'm supposed to go up there now and talk to her. She says she's suspended you. What's got into you anyway?"

"I didn't steal the watch, Dad. It was planted on me, I swear."

"Charlie, you're not living in the real world. Why would anyone plant a watch on you? It was found in your desk, wasn't it?"

I bent down and started to undo the laces of my muddy shoes. At least I wouldn't have Granny Bea on my case for messing up the carpet.

"Charlie, are you listening to me? Because I want to get to the bottom of this. I won't have any daughter of mine nicking stuff. And look at the state of that coat, will you? Do you think I'm made of money?"

"No," I shook my head. "I didn't mean to rip it, honestly."

"Get out of those clothes and then come down to the kitchen, do you hear? This is costing me real money—I've had to take time off to come home early and see about all this."

I slunk upstairs. As I was changing into clean clothes, I made up my mind to tell him everything, how they bullied me and called me the Abandoned Baby. He would have to listen to me, then. He'd clear my name. He might even let me go to a different school. Maybe, I thought, as I dabbed the blood from my legs, maybe it would turn out for the best that all this had happened. We could talk about what happened in London, how I remembered everything. He could tell me where my mother was.

As I came down the stairs again, I could hear Dad and Noel talking in the kitchen.

"I'm not surprised her mother dumped her," my dad was saying. "She'd try the patience of a saint."

I let myself out the door and closed it quietly behind me.

6

RUNAWAY

I walked and walked, not knowing where I was going and not caring. All I wanted was to be on my own. No, I didn't even want to be on my own. Depression hung over me like a black cloud. I hated myself and everybody I knew.

I dragged myself along the streets crying, I think, some of the time, or at least sobbing and making little animal noises. No one spoke to me. I felt absolutely exhausted but I made myself keep on going, putting one foot in front of the other. What has this world got to offer me, I was thinking. Nothing. I didn't want to be part of it.

I thought about killing myself. What would be the best, the quickest, the least painful way of doing it? I could just go back home, I thought, and take all the paracetamol in the bathroom—but would there be enough? How long would it take? If you didn't take enough to kill yourself, could you be brain-damaged? I hated the thought of surviving but with all the intelligence of a turnip, perhaps not being able to talk, having to wear nappies. I couldn't bear to give Lorna and the rest of them that satisfaction. I thought about cutting my wrists but I didn't think I'd have the nerve. Even if I managed to draw the blade across one wrist, I couldn't see myself passing the knife to the other hand and doing it a second time. Drowning would be easier. You sometimes read in the papers about people walking into the cold grey sea at Dún Laoghaire—often the body wasn't washed up for days. I had this horrible picture of a body, swollen and bloated from weeks in the water, being picked at by small darting silver fish. No, I couldn't drown myself either.

I just wanted to be dead, not to have to die.

I had walked miles by this time and was coming down a hill where I could see the whole curve of Dublin Bay. The lights of the city had come on but the chimneys of the Pigeon House were still belching out their plumes of white smoke. They drifted across the deserted strand of Sandymount in the direction of the blue-grey mound of Howth Head. The air felt thick and heavy and dirty. It was pitch dark and the streets were quite deserted and still. The only noise was the sound of my own footsteps falling on the pavement. I turned into a park and climbed up a steep path to where I knew there was a bench. My body was so tired I could hardly walk straight, but more than that, my heart and my brain were tired. I wanted to shut down, to go to sleep and never wake up.

I thought about my mother, wondering if she was somewhere out there, if she ever thought of me. I could see her face so sharply in my mind still, and wished she would come and find me. Why wasn't she looking after me, I thought bitterly, when I needed her most. How could she have done such a wicked thing, abandoning me in that station all those years ago? Was I really so hateful? Didn't she know I might have been killed? Didn't she know a thing like that could screw someone up for the rest of their life? What made her so sure that Dad would be willing to come and get me? Did she ever find out what happened to me? She'd be sorry, they'd all be sorry, when my body was found, dead of a broken heart.

I don't think I could have slept long—it was too cold and uncomfortable—but I probably dozed off for a few minutes. The next thing I knew a dog was standing in front of me, prodding me with its front paws. A great wave of despair flooded over me when I realised I was still alive. I wanted to scream at God to stop messing me about. I pushed the dog away and stood up. It made a low whining noise, hurt that I had rejected it. I sat down again, buried my head in its head and let it lick my wet tearful face.

"What's the matter, kid?"

I looked up. It was the boy from the bus stop, the boy who had pulled me off the road when I walked out in front of the bread van. I sniffed and tried to stop sobbing but my shoulders kept shaking.

"You lost?" he said.

I shook my head, hoping he would go away and leave me alone but he just stood there, looking down on the top of my head. I wiped my eyes and stared at the laces on his docs. The dog looked from one to the other of us.

"You in trouble?"

I shook my head from side to side but kept my eyes on his shoes.

"Have you run away?"

I must have given a little nod.

"Got any money?"

I said nothing.

"Come on," he said, "you look freezing. I'll buy you a cup of tea."

The dog followed us out of the park, over the railway bridge and down to the beach road where a man in a manky-looking caravan was selling hamburgers and drinks. Casso paid for two teas and stuffed a big handful of sugar lumps in his pocket when the man had his back turned. I sat on a rock facing out to sea and warmed my hands around the plastic cup while Casso threw lumps of sugar up in the air for the dog to jump and catch.

"Was it those girls again?" he said after a while. I didn't answer. The dog was barking and going crazy, running about the beach in circles, trying to catch its own tail.

"You don't have to tell me if you don't want to, it's up to you.

But it's no weather for sleeping rough." He took the lid off the cup and threw it out to sea.

"You shouldn't do that," I said.

"Says who and whose army?" he said and gave me a grin. "Go on, spill the beans. What did you do?"

"I didn't do anything," I said, indignantly. "It was those bloody creeps."

Casso was a good listener. He was the first person who had really listened to me for years and years. And he didn't ask me stupid questions like why I let them get away with it...

I told him everything, right from the time in the first term when Lorna started calling me the Abandoned Baby.

"Why do they you call you that?"

So I had to start again right back when my mother abandoned me in London and how I thought no one knew about it.

"Even my dad doesn't know I remember."

"And they pick on you for that?"

"They say it means I'm hateful, that even my mother couldn't stand me. They freeze me out so that no one in the whole class will be my friend. They scribble on my copy-books and tell lies about me. And they spit at me and say I stole a watch and they're always setting me up in front of the teachers."

"Sounds like you're having a rough time."

"And then the worst thing is I think my dad knows where my mum is—he might send me back to her."

Casso sucked in his breath and made a little whistle. "Naw, Charlie, he wouldn't do that."

"He hates me. He doesn't want me around. If it wasn't for Granny, he probably would put me in care or something."

"Of course he wouldn't, Charlie. You're just being melo-dramatic."

Then I told him what I had overheard my dad saying to Noel in the kitchen. "That's why I ran away."

Casso finished the rest of his tea and squashed the cup

between clenched fingers. We both listened to the sea dragging the pebbles back and forth along the shore.

"Your parents are something else, aren't they?" he said after a bit. "What do you want to do, then?"

"I don't know—but I'm not going home—and I'm not going back to that school either." My lip might have trembled but my mind was made up.

"Well, you can't sleep rough. You're too young and you haven't even got a coat—Jesus, it's freezing cold already and it's not even six o'clock. What do you think it'll be like at two o'clock in the morning? Is there nowhere else you could go? Have you any other relatives?"

I shrugged. The whole point was I didn't want to see anybody I knew. They had all let me down.

"You'd better come home with me then. With any luck, no one will even notice one extra for tea."

Casso stood up and whistled for the dog to come back to him. "Murphy, come on Murphy, attaboy."

The red setter came rushing out of the sea, scattering drops of water in every direction, and ran barking to his side. Without a second thought, I followed them off the beach.

Casso's house was jammed with people. There was a circle of kids on the sitting-room floor eating fish fingers and watching television. There were two men and two women playing cards at the table in the front room. From upstairs came the sound of someone thrashing chords on an electric lead guitar. Two more men were standing at the kitchen table, one of them big and soft with a round cheerful face, the other equally tall but sharp and lean, like an older Casso. They were counting parcels of what looked like sweaters wrapped in polythene and packing them into boxes.

Every so often, the soft one shuffled off with a laden box and added it to the stack in the hall. I had already noticed boxes everywhere, in the porch, on the kitchen table, piled up on the sofa, on the sideboard, stacked behind the door.

"Hi ya, Casso," said one of the men. "Ma's looking for you. You missed your tea."

Casso lit a match under a battered old saucepan on the cooker and took out a bag of potatoes from under the sink.

"Here," he said to me, "peel us a few spuds for chips while I feed Murphy."

He caught the dog by the collar and half-dragged it out of the room. I could hear them go downstairs. A door banged.

I looked around me in embarrassment, feeling deserted.

"Don't mind us, darling," said the fat man. "We've eaten already."

I began to peel the potatoes, letting the hot water run over my freezing hands. After a while I forgot to be embarrassed about cooking my own supper in a stranger's house.

"This young girl's a friend of yours, Casso, is she?" said the fat man when Casso came back into the room.

"Yeah," said Casso, "she's having a bit of trouble at home."

"What kind of trouble?" said the Casso lookalike. "I hope it's not what I'm thinking."

"For God's sake, Dekko," said Casso, looking at me and giving me a sort of embarrassed grin. "Nothing like that—there was a bit of trouble at school and her dad flipped his lid."

"What's your name, darling?"

"Charlie, Charlotte Collins."

"You don't live around here, do you, Charlie?"

I shook my head. "Florence Road," I said.

The two men resumed their packing, noisily tearing off strips of sticky tape to seal the boxes. Casso cut up the potatoes I had peeled and we stood silently side by side in front of the cooker, looking at the bubbling fat in the chip pan. When they were cooked, Casso divided the chips on to two plates and sprinkled them with salt and vinegar.

"Right," said Dekko, when we were stuck into eating, "you'd

better tell us what's going on here."

He pulled up a kitchen chair and sat down on it, back to front. His arms, resting on the back of the chair, were hard and muscular, covered in fine black hair.

"Charlie just needs a bit of a break. She's being hassled at school, bullied. Somebody said she stole a watch and got her suspended. And now her dad doesn't believe her."

"What about your mum?" asked Dekko.

"I haven't got one," I said, which was simpler than telling the truth, and wasn't a lie in any case.

"Does your dad work in Magee's pub? Peter Collins, right?" I nodded.

"Right, thought I recognised the name. You kids stay here until we get back. Make yourselves a cup of tea. Come on, Triggs, I'll buy you a pint."

The second man grinned happily and pushed the last cardboard box under the kitchen table.

"Who are they?" I asked when they had gone out.

"My brothers, Declan and Francis, or Dekko and Trigger."

"Why's he called Trigger?"

"Think about it. He's not the fastest gun in the west for sure."

"Have you any sisters?"

Casso snorted with laughter. "You got to be kidding. There's sixteen of us, eight boys and eight girls."

I gaped at him. Sixteen children! I couldn't imagine what it was like to have even one brother or sister, let alone fifteen.

"Do they all live here?" I asked.

"Most of them, on and off. Some of them are in America, some in England. They kind of come and go."

"Do you all hang around together all the time?"

"No way!" said Casso, emphatically. "That's why I like to clear off with Murphy, to get away from all the noise and carry-on in this house."

"And your mum and dad?"

"Nosey little thing, aren't you?"

I blushed and finished my tea. "I'd better go home."

"Naw, it's okay. Take your time. The old lady's probably out shopping. The da's down the country somewhere. He has a van. Sells stuff at markets. That's what all the boxes of sweaters are for."

Before I could ask any more questions, the front door opened and I heard a familiar voice coming down the hall. It was Dad.

He came into the kitchen, with Dekko at his heels and Trigger behind that, his big moonface wreathed in smiles. Dad gave me an awkward sort of hug.

"Jesus, Charlie, you gave us all an awful fright. Your granny's been going mad with worry." His face looked flushed and worried. He smelt and sounded as if he had been drinking but that might just have been from the smell of the pub where he worked.

We walked home together, arms linked, bouncing along briskly with false heartiness as if we were just an ordinary dad and daughter out for a late evening stroll. Neither of us wanted to speak and break the fragile truce between us. Both of us were happy to pretend that everything was all right now. At Granny's front door, before we went inside, Dad caught my wrist and said, "Before we go in, Charlie, will you do me a favour?"

I waited while he pulled out his stupid cigarette packet and slowly lit one.

"Just don't say where you were to your granny or the others," he said finally.

"Why not?"

"They're a rough lot round there in the flats. Granny wouldn't like it. Don't get involved with that shower, okay?"

I shrugged.

"I've had to ban that Dekko once or twice from the pub, you know. As for that Trigger—he's the one that got me in trouble over a dodgy baked potato. I don't want you mixed up with his

42

kid brother."

I pretended to be looking for my key in my pockets so that I didn't have to look at him. Casso was the nicest person I knew.

"And another thing, Charlie—about what happened this morning—did you steal the watch?"

"No," I said, angrily. "I told you. The girl planted it on me. They all hate me there."

"I'll go up with you to the school tomorrow and sort it all out." He gave me a peck on the cheek. "I didn't mean it, Charlie—what I said to Noel in the kitchen. That is why you ran away, isn't it?" His voice broke as if he was going to break down and cry. "I don't know what got into me. I was just freaked out. You know I didn't mean it, don't you?" He pressed the heels of his hands into his eyes and sniffed loudly. "You'll understand when you're a bit older, the pressures I'm under." His voice petered out.

I gave him a peck back and walked ahead of him to turn the key in the lock. For the first time I had just seen my dad for what he was, a weak man, a man who could let you down. One thing was certain—he hadn't a clue about the pressures I was under. In that instant between opening the door and crossing the threshold, I felt that life had just shunted me into another track. Things between us would never be the same again.

7

NO FURTHER CAUSE FOR
CONCERN

The following morning I heard the alarm clock go off in the bedroom next to mine. I lay in bed, sleepily listening to all the early morning sounds of the house, wondering whether I should get up or not. The radio came on in Granny's room, the boiler flared as someone ran a shower, a loo flushed, teacups rattled downstairs. The smell of toast seeped under the door of my room. Any moment Dad would call me and let me know what time he was taking me to the school.

Feet ran down and up the stairs. Noel and Vinnie left the house with a shout of farewell and a loud bang of the front door that shook the mirror of my dressing-table and sent Gary Gatwick slipping off the window-sill. The house became so still that I thought I must be alone. I put on my dressing-gown and went downstairs. In the kitchen, Granny, tight-lipped, was standing at the kitchen sink, noisily rinsing cups and banging them down on the drainer. You could have cut the atmosphere with the bread knife.

"Is Dad up yet, Granny?"

She dried her hands on the tea towel and turned to me with a false bright smile.

"Your dad can't go to see your headmistress after all, Charlie love. He left with the others. If you get yourself dressed, I'll take you."

It was pretty obvious that Granny and Dad must have had a row. I might have known that Dad would chicken out. I'll sort it out, he had said. Even if he had meant it at the time, his good intentions had melted away overnight. In the end, he probably convinced himself I'd like to have the week off and that the whole episode would have blown over by the time I went back to school.

"I've nothing to wear, Granny. My uniform's wrecked," I said.

"How come?"

I told her how Lorna had dropped my bag on the railway track. I made it sound more of an accident than it was. I didn't say anything about the trains.

We drove to school with the radio on in the car. There was a phone-in programme. A woman with a terrible voice was singing birthday greetings to her mother. Granny abruptly switched it off. She got nervous when people talked about their mothers.

"Aren't there other girls you can pal around with?" she asked. She was wearing a bright smear of orangey lipstick and the black beret she always wore for church, which made her look unfamiliar, out of character. Anyone who saw her might think she was my mother.

"I suppose so," I said. "Don't tell anyone about them throwing my schoolbag on the railway line. It'll just make things worse."

✳✳✳

We stood in front of the secretary's desk and waited for her to finish a phone call. Granny refused to take a seat or have a cup of coffee. She didn't have much time, she said. She said grandly that she was a busy woman with a business to look after but the secretary looked anything but impressed. Eventually she waved a hand towards the door of the inner office.

"The principal will see you now."

I was following behind but Granny turned and stopped me.

"No, Charlie, you wait here for the moment. This won't take long."

The secretary told me to go and sit by the window. Immediately I began to worry about what was going on in the other office. I strained to hear if there were raised voices. I should never have told Granny anything. If Lorna and the others guessed that I had grassed on them, my life wouldn't be worth living. I began tearing at the roots of my nails and tugging at the loose skin until my fingers bled. On the other side of the room, the secretary, making no effort to conceal her contempt for me, pretended to read the morning's post but I could see she was really eavesdropping on the conversation next door.

After what seemed like an eternity, there was a flurry of phone calls. The secretary prepared a tray of coffee and biscuits and took it in. Shortly afterwards, she announced over the loudspeaker that Tara Lennon was to come to the office. Tara came in smiling, unconcerned until she saw me. A few minutes later, the door opened again and Granny came out. The head shook her hand and held on to it, assuring her she would be in touch again soon, that there was no further cause for concern.

"My dear Charlotte," she said, turning to me and putting her arm around my shoulder as if I was absolutely one of her most favoured pupils, "it seems we owe you an apology. However, I hope we'll all be able to put this distasteful episode behind us. Now off you go to class."

"Nice woman," said Granny when we went outside.

"Mmmm," I said.

Later on, Tara, tear-stained, came into our form room and emptied her locker.

By lunch-time the news was out—Tara had been expelled.

I dreaded to think what that would mean for me.

NO FURTHER CAUSE FOR CONCERN

***

At morning assembly the next day, the head gave a talk on bullying and said the school would not tolerate it in any shape or form. Whatever measures, no matter how severe, that she thought necessary would be taken to eradicate it. No girl should think twice of reporting anyone involved in it. No girl should put up with degrading treatment. The teachers were there to help us. They would be tireless in rooting out bad influences. The school was proud of its record as a caring community. We must all pull together to build on that reputation. And more along the same lines.

There were a few shame-faced overtures of friendship towards me after that but nothing radical changed in the days that followed. Lorna and her cronies were more subdued than usual. They still snubbed me but I had the sensation that they were just biding their time to take their revenge. The knowledge that Tara's expulsion was all my fault and that they would forever hold it against me hung over me like a hangman's noose that was bound to tighten around my neck one day.

8

REFLECTIONS AND
RECOLLECTIONS

I stared at my reflection in the mirror every night and tried to understand the face that looked back at me. At times it seemed to have no connection with what I thought I looked like, as if my brain, my self had got locked into the wrong body. I hated her, this other girl whose brown eyes bore into mine. She was too thin, her face too pale and hollow. I fingered the stubbly patches on the top of her skull where the black hair she had pulled out by the handful was just starting to grow back. I traced the shape of her mouth with my index finger, feeling the full bottom lip, dry and cracked now from the February wind. I would sometimes bend forward and kiss her, my warm mouth leaving behind a steamy imprint on the cold mirror. We practised smiling at one another but there was no love behind the smile. There were times as I turned my head away from her, I fancied I saw over my shoulder an older face looking back at me.

In the evenings after tea, I watched my dad and the uncles while they sat looking at television. They all had the same very light brown hair. (Granny's hair was blonder with grey streaks but she didn't count, for her colour, I knew, came out of a bottle.) All the Collins family had straight hair without a single kink in it, completely different from mine which escaped in dark-black curly wisps around my forehead no matter how often I scraped it back into a pony-tail. For as long as I could remember, Dad,

Noel and Vinnie had worn the same style, short and parted to one side. It was the kind of hair that didn't move—it looked the same all day, as neat and smooth as when they first combed it. It was like spray-on hair. I decided I must look like my mother.

The idea appalled me. If I looked like her, was I like her in other ways? Was I the sort of person who could walk away from a child in the middle of a big city, with no more protection than a phone number in her pocket? I began to probe my brain for other memories of her, forcing myself back in time to the years I lived with her in London, terrified at what I might remember but driven on by the need to know her, to know what kind of person had given birth to me.

I began to have dreams, nightmares in which I wandered lost among rushing strangers but everyone I spoke to to ask for directions would turn out to have Lorna's face and would scream at me not to make a fuss, to find my own way. In another dream, I was in a court-room, in the dock. A voice read out the list of my crimes.

"You are the Abandoned Baby." Guilty.

"You are a bastard." Guilty.

"You hate your mother." Guilty.

"You grass on your best friends." Guilty.

"You are a coward." Guilty.

I had other dreams too, dreams of what I supposed was London. Once I woke in the middle of the night, frightened and bathed in sweat. I couldn't shake off the image of a dingy unfurnished room. A young blonde woman with dark roots lay on the mattress in one corner of the room. She had rolled up the sleeve of her shirt above her elbow, and was tying a scarf around her arm in a tight knot. A young child, a girl I knew to be me, whimpered at the door. Turning her back on the child, the woman pushed a needle into the pulsing vein. "Don't make a fuss, Charlie," she said, slipping back on the heap of dirty pillows. "Come and sit here beside me and comb my hair."

✳✳✳

"Dad," I said at breakfast the next morning. "Was my mum blonde or dark like me?"

He looked up at me, aghast, with that same frightened look on his face that he had had the day we were doing the lottery tickets and he said Lisa's name.

"What brought this on?" he said, feeling in his pockets for the cigarette packet.

"Your hair is light brown, nearly fair. Mine is very dark."

Dad looked around over his shoulder guiltily, as if worried we might be overheard.

"She was blonde most of the time I knew her—but it wasn't natural." He lit a cigarette and blew out the smoke slowly. "Look, Charlie, leave well alone, eh, that's a girl. There's no point in raking over the past. What's done is done."

"What age was I when you came back here?" I insisted. "Why did Lisa and I not come with you? Did you walk out on us? Did you abandon us first? Is that why she dumped me? She was just using me to take her revenge on you?"

"Jesus, Charlie, what is this?" He stood up and began to move dishes over to the sink. "It's too complicated to explain. It all happened a long time ago."

"What age was I?" I repeated. He was going to talk about it.

"Two," he said, at last, "it was just after your second birthday." He paused for a few moments, staring into the distance as if trying to summon up memories that he had buried a long time ago. "We were living in a house in Shepherd's Bush, a terrible dump to be honest. I'd just failed my exams at college but I didn't want to go back to Dublin. I didn't need the grief I knew I'd get from the old lady so I just stayed on in England and didn't go back for the resits. In any case nobody back in Dublin knew about Lisa and me. I mean, nobody knew Lisa had had a kid." He looked at me distractedly and reached out his hand to take mine.

"Nobody knew we had you. Jesus, we must have been out of our heads, keeping a thing like that secret. Lisa had been in London all the time she was pregnant and I came over during the holidays. She didn't want anyone to know.

"Anyway, I was working in one of those new American ice-cream parlours the summer I failed the exams. Ginger snap and blueberry, pistachio and double cranberry crunch, flavours nobody had ever heard of before. Lisa used to bring you in sometimes when we were a bit slack and I'd give you little tubs of whatever colour you wanted. I talked about getting married, settling down.

"One Sunday morning, I woke up and you were both gone. No note, nothing. Lisa had done a bunk."

Dad stopped talking and stared out the window into the garden. A ginger cat was stealthily padding along the top of the fence, stalking a blackbird in the cherry tree. He watched it in silence while I watched him, terrified that he would not finish the story. I had never heard him talk like this before.

"At first I thought she'd just gone out to the shops but hours passed and she hadn't got back. I began to worry. I was afraid that she might have taken something." Dad looked up at me, as if remembering who he was talking to. "She did drugs, Charlie. I was afraid she might do something stupid with you if I didn't find her. I went out and walked around the streets. I remember going over to Notting Hill on the tube. Lisa had a couple of mates who lived in a squat there but they didn't know anything. I rang a couple of hospitals, but of course they couldn't tell me anything either.

"I waited for three weeks in that sodding house, afraid to go out in case you came back and I wasn't there, waiting for the key to turn. In the end I knew she wasn't coming back. I took the train to Holyhead and caught the ferry back here."

"Did you find out what happened? Have you ever heard from her? Do you know where she is now? You do, don't you?" I thought of the square yellow piece of paper which he had folded into his pocket, the paper with the word LISA written in sloping letters.

Dad stubbed out his cigarette, slowly grinding away at it.

"You're late for school," he said, at last. "You'd better get a move on."

"But Dad," I began.

"No, Charlie, that's it. The next thing I knew was more than two years later, when the police rang to say they had found you in Victoria, that you had been abandoned. She had put a letter and a telephone number in your pocket. Now go on, pet, go to school."

9

THE PHOTOGRAPH

Piecing together my life before I was brought to Dublin was the only thing I wanted to do after that. If you don't know your own history, you don't know who you are. I felt as if a great chunk of myself was missing, or at least, hidden behind locked doors, and I became obsessed with finding it. At school, I daydreamed all the time about those missing years, the time between Dad leaving London and the day I was dumped. Where had I been? Who had I been with? The only person who could answer those questions was Lisa—but how was I going to find her? I didn't even know for sure if she was in Ireland. I could have got it all wrong about the name on the telephone notepad. Dad could have been talking to anybody. All the stress at school was making me imagine conspiracies everywhere.

I had to keep remembering that Lisa had got rid of me once—even if I did find out where she was, she might not want me reappearing in her life. She might be married now, with another family. Or she might be dead.

"Charlotte Collins! What planet are you on these days? That's the third time I've had to call your name."

I leapt to my feet with a start as Mrs Armstrong came bearing down on me. Thirty faces wheeled around to stare at me, grateful for a little light relief from working out the area of a hexagon. I sat down again quickly, feeling a fool and looked around me in dismay, wondering helplessly what I was supposed to say. Mrs Armstrong's lumpy bosom bent over me. She smelled of wool and heavy unpleasant perfume.

"Your calculations have gone haywire," she said, drawing a red line across my page with a theatrical flourish. "I might as well have been talking to a cabbage for all the attention I'm getting." The class tittered. Mrs Armstrong shook her head at me, looking at me as if I was brain-damaged.

"Day-dreaming again, Miss Collins? What was it this time— an island in the sun? castles in Spain? It's about time you knuckled down to a bit of work, young lady."

I cast my eyes down, letting the wave of abuse wash over me but all the time I was thinking, Charlotte Collins. It had never occurred to me before, but Collins was Dad's name. It wasn't Lisa's name. That was where I had to start. I could hardly wait to get home.

I threw my bag under the stairs and headed for the kitchen. Noel, Vinnie and Granny were all sitting around the table drinking coffee and doing the Simplex crossword.

"Bird raises heavy weight?" Vinnie was reading out.

"Crane," said Granny.

"Great! Now four down begins with n, seven letters, Mandarin's spaghetti."

"Listen," I said, "do I have a birth certificate?"

Granny raised her head slowly from the newspaper and pressed her lips together so hard they completely disappeared.

"Noodles," said Noel.

"Why?" Granny asked.

"The Chinese spaghetti," said Noel.

Granny shook her head angrily at him and asked me again. "Why do you want to know about a birth certificate? Did they ask for it at school?"

"I just want to know if I have one," I said.

Granny looked at Noel and Vinnie. Vinnie shrugged.

"What's the harm?" he said. "Peter must have had to get one for her some time, maybe when she started school. It would be a British one, wouldn't it, seeing as how she was born in London?" He turned to me. "Ask your dad. He'll be home soon."

But I couldn't wait to ask my dad. I crept into his room and began to search the top drawer of his dressing-table where I had often seen him throw papers and bills and official-looking letters. I had to be really quiet for I knew I would be killed if anyone came into the room and saw what I was doing.

Dad certainly held on to the most incredible junk—ancient yellowing payslips, books of matches from nightclubs in town, old airline tickets, a Fathers' Day card I had made him when I was about six, cassette tapes with no boxes, leaky pens and empty cigarette packets, the man was a pig. I rooted about, getting quite carried away—I found his Leaving Certificate and his passport (with a photograph that made him look like a convicted criminal) but no birth certificate. I was just about to give up when I saw the packet of photographs.

Until then I had never noticed that about this family: no one ever took photographs. In fact I don't think anybody even owned a camera. Apart from the awful photos they took at school every year, I hadn't got a single snapshot of myself. The photos turned out to be a real mixture, all taken at different times, all shapes and sizes. There were ones of Dad and all my uncles when they were small, there was one of Granny at someone else's wedding and a man that I supposed was my grandfather. There were school photos of Dad, looking thin and gangly in a basketball team. Then there were more recent ones— Dad grinning on a bridge with the Eiffel Tower behind him, loads of tanned smiling faces sitting around a table in some hot country, bottles and glasses everywhere.

Last of all, there was the photo that made my heart stop. Dad and me, I thought, but then I realised the girl was about twenty. It was just that she had my face.

55

Downstairs I heard the front door opening. With no time to spare, I pushed the photographs back into their envelope, slid the drawer closed and tiptoed into my own room next door. But the photograph of my mother and father, I did not put back. I put that in my pocket.

Lying on my tummy on my bed, I took the picture out and laid it on the pillow in front of me. At first I couldn't bear to look directly at her. I was so nervous my hands were shaking. I slowly examined every square millimetre of that snap before I could bring myself to look properly at her face. Dad had his arm tight around her shoulder and was looking directly into the camera. He looked younger, healthy, not as thin as he is now, not frowning the way he mostly does now. He was wearing a big thick blue anorak and jeans. Behind him were high snowy mountains—it had to be the time he was in Canada. Could it have been the day they saw the bear?

Lisa was small and thin, barely up to his shoulder. Her face was tilted up as if she had just looked up to say something to him. It was then I realised that, once upon a time, they had loved one another, loved each other long enough to stay together for years and have me. Because she had been written out of my family history for so long, that had never occurred to me. I had never heard my father say her name, or laughing, remember a time we were all together. It was worse than if she had died—at least people would have spoken about her—but she had done the unspeakable and so had to be cut out of my life, her existence denied.

I looked at her face and tried to figure out how I felt about her. I was touched by the way she was looking up at my father, by her smallness, but I still hated her. This was the woman who could leave a small child in the middle of a huge railway station and just walk away. This was the selfish cruel bitch who had made me, who hadn't loved me, who was able to cast me aside like a discarded newspaper. This was the face that had bent down over me and said, Charlie, don't make a fuss, and had then walked away out of my life without a backward glance. But I wanted her too, I wanted to know her, I wanted her to love me. Tears rolled down my cheeks, my nose began to run, my whole body shook with uncontrollable sobbing. I thought my heart would break.

BULLY OFF

10

BULLY OFF

For a while after I had run away, Dad and I settled into an uneasy truce. Most of the time we ignored one another. I guess he was embarrassed that he had let me down by not going to the school with me after I was suspended, and ashamed that he had let Granny go in his place. We ducked around the house, trying to avoid being in the same room together. I even stopped doing the lottery with him on Saturday afternoons, so that I didn't have to put on that silly act of saying what we'd do if we won—but he didn't seem to notice. In the end, there were days when we didn't see each other at all.

Even Granny seemed to have drawn a veil over the trouble at school, content to think it had all ended happily. Nobody mentioned I'd been asking for my birth certificate, at least not in my hearing. I hated them all, for brushing everything under the carpet, for covering up my past, for being afraid. If I had been adopted by complete strangers, they would probably have told me more about my past. But all I could look forward to were more walls of silence.

I still dreaded going to school. Hardly a day went past without Lorna and Natalie setting out to hurt me with their small-minded cruelties and spiteful remarks but I was learning, or I thought I was. I practised drifting outside myself, looking down on the classroom as if watching a scene from a play in which I had no part at all. The Abandoned Baby was not me. I grew deaf to the remarks they flung at her. I was cold and unmoved by her pain.

Even weeks after Tara's expulsion, as the winter ended and spring arrived, the class still talked about what had happened. She, after all, had been at that school for years and I was a nobody—and a sneak, according to her friends. Grassing was the ultimate crime: no matter what they had done to me, I should have kept my mouth shut. I had broken the secret code of honour that says, whatever happens, don't tell. What right had I to expect anything but their scorn? I had only myself to blame if I was unpopular now, hated not only by Lorna and her cronies but distrusted by everyone in the school.

A few of the teachers, however, knew something was not right. They could probably feel the underlying air of menace in our room, like in one of those horror films on television where things might seem all right on the surface but a lunatic with an axe is hiding in the next block, bent on revenge. I watched them watching me, looking for signs of trouble. The problem was they handled it all wrong. Where before I had been the butt of all their sarcasm, labelled as the class loser even by the staff, now they singled me out for special attention. It was clear that everyone knew about my secret shameful past, that I was the Abandoned Baby, so they handled me with kid gloves. If I was by myself at break-time—and I usually was—some well-meaning adult would come and talk to me. In front of the whole class, they would tell me I was looking a bit peaky and should eat more. If I did any work that was half-way decent, it would be praised lavishly. "Well done, Charlotte. I'm so glad to see you working well." I could hear the sniggers, see the wide-eyed looks of disbelief. I became even quieter, keeping my head down, protecting myself from harm. I was not surprised to hear voices behind my back calling me teacher's pet, a lick, and a two-faced little bitch. I knew I would have to pay for it.

Lorna had to develop more devious ways of punishing me, of getting her own back, doing petty, mean things which nobody could blame on her. Since Tara had left, Monica had been admitted into Lorna and Natalie's inner circle, and brought a cruder element to their games. Once I opened my desk and found a great gobbet of spit on my books. I said nothing.

Later the same day, we had double art. This was my favourite subject and the art room my favourite room in the whole school. It was a big light room with windows on three sides, overlooking the building site where they were putting up the new classrooms and science block. I had just finished a painting and had placed it on the big trestle-table at the back to dry. I stood back to admire it—it showed a workman on a yellow mechanical digger gouging out the hole for the foundations. The black mound of topsoil was strewn with pink blossom from the cherry trees outside the art-room window. It was the best composition I had ever done, Mr Nelson said, good enough to go on the wall.

"Charlotte's turning into a boffin, as if that will do her any good," Natalie whispered loud enough for me to hear as I passed the table where she was working with Lorna.

"I know, it's pathetic. Everyone knows the little bastard's dad is only a barman."

We started to tidy up at the end of the lesson. Everyone was on the move around the room, emptying the jam-jars of dirty water, cleaning brushes, wiping smears of paint from table tops. I found my painting again. It was on the ground, trampled and dirty, the pink and white blossom stamped on by a pair of muddy ridged soles.

"Don't make such a fuss," said Mr Nelson, "you can do it again. Cheer up."

But I knew from the guilty silence that hung over the rest of the class and the way they made sidelong glances at Lorna that this was no accident.

If I had had any support from the others, things might have

been different, but I felt completely alone, like a piece of stinking dog mess that was so repugnant no one could bear to be near. The worst thing wasn't what they did to me, it was not having any friends, of being pushed away all the time, being made to feel invisible. I felt completely worthless as I trudged along the corridor towards the dining-hall for lunch.

The other girls hurried ahead of me, arms linked, pushing to get clear of the crowds. They knocked into other pupils going in the opposite direction, reluctantly coming back from first lunch.

"Mind where you're going, stupid."

"Mind yourself."

I stood in line, waiting to get to the counter. I was wedged between two groups of third years from other classes. They eyed me curiously, as if afraid I was going to tag along with them, and moved closer together, turning their backs on me.

"What's for dessert?" said one of the bolder ones.

"Abandoned Baby."

"What?"

"Apple Charlotte!"

There was a loud explosion of laughter and all the heads turned to look at me. I looked down at the floor, examining the scuffed black and white tiles. Voices filled the room, laughing and chattering. Everyone had someone to talk to except me.

"All right," I thought. "That's it. I'll get you all. I've nothing left to lose."

***

Last lesson was sports. From my point of view the hockey game might as well have been played on another pitch. I spent the whole time running backwards and forwards, but no one ever passed me the ball. I had Lorna shadowing me and she just never gave an inch. All the action was down at the other goal in any case. The blues were winning eight-nil when suddenly, the hockey ball seemed to come out of nowhere, rolling towards myself and Lorna. I saw my chance. There was a loud thud as our sticks clashed and locked together, both of us trying to gain possession.

Suddenly Monica was at my side, deliberately hitting out at my ankles. I let out a yelp at the pain and stepped back, raising my stick slightly to take better aim at the ball. At the same time, Lorna appeared to lose her balance and slip in the muddy grass. There was a loud crack but Monica had the ball. She raced away from us, deftly steering the ball and racing with it towards the net. The blues cheered, nine-nil. The whistle blew.

Lorna's body lay crumpled in the mud. A trickle of blood bubbled from her open mouth.

I threw my stick to the ground and shouted for help, though no words would come out. My voice sounded strangled and hoarse, too weak to rise above the cheers of the winning team. I shouted again and knelt down beside the motionless body at my feet.

"Stand back, stand back." Mrs O'Byrne, the games teacher, was kneeling by my side. "Give the girl some space. Lorna, are you all right? Lorna, can you hear me?"

Lorna did not move. A purple bruise was spreading darkly on the side of her forehead.

Mrs O'Byrne gently pushed back the hair from Lorna's face. With her other hand she felt for a pulse at her neck.

"It was Charlie, miss," said a voice. "She hit her on the head with her stick."

"It wasn't like that," I protested.

"Stop it, will you? Rachel and Monica, go to the office and tell them to call an ambulance. Tell them it's an emergency. Hurry. The rest of you go to the gym and wait there until I come."

"She tripped in the mud," I said. "I didn't do it deliberately. My stick just caught the side of her head when she slipped."

"It's not true, miss. She hates Lorna. Everybody knows that."

"I saw it too, miss. Natalie is right. Is Lorna dead?"

The teacher unzipped the top of her track suit and placed it over Lorna's still body.

"Enough!" she said. "I'll talk to you later. Now go to the gym, all of you."

I trailed bleakly behind as the class crossed the playing field towards the gymnasium. The image of Lorna's cold bruised face and the trickle of blood from her mouth would not leave me. I felt very scared. As we approached the main building, the head teacher came running down the steps, her black gown blowing out like a sail behind her, a look of blind terror on her face.

"Where are they?" she called out, without stopping.

"On the pitch, the far end. Please miss, Charlie did it."

The head turned her head briefly towards me but kept on running. In the far distance we could hear the strident siren of an ambulance approaching.

There were already mutterings in the gym when I entered. Natalie was in tears, surrounded by a crowd of sympathisers...

"First she lied about Tara and had her expelled. Now she's gone and half-killed Lorna. What has she got against me and my friends? It'll be me next." Her shoulders shook with sobbing.

Monica put an arm around her. "Don't worry, Nat. We'll look after you."

"She's mental!" said another voice and all the others chorused in turn.

"Well, she won't get away with it this time. They'll have to get rid of her now."

"She ought to be locked up."

"I hate the way she licks up to all the teachers. She must think we're all idiots."

"She's evil. No wonder her mother dumped her."

"It was an accident," I shouted. "She slipped in the mud. Monica saw what happened."

"Some accident! I saw you whacking her in the head,"

Monica retorted.

"She was already on the ground when you hit her."

"That's not true!" I shouted again. "It wasn't my fault."

Monica moved towards me and gave me a shove back towards the wall. "We don't want you in here. Get out."

"No," I said. "You can't do that."

"Oh yes, we can," the others started up and all of them advanced towards me, their faces contorted with hatred and contempt.

I backed towards the wall. They kept coming towards me. Someone pushed my shoulder, then someone else took hold of my hair and yanked it down so fiercely, it brought tears to my eyes.

"Look, she's crying. The Abandoned Baby's going to blub."

I felt a kick in my shins, then another and another. They were prodding me, poking at me, swarming all around like a pack of jackals with a cornered prey, the smell of blood in their nostrils.

"Leave me alone," I screamed, covering my head with my hands. This time the tears were real.

The siren of the ambulance screeched. We could hear it brake to a halt, scattering the loose gravel on the avenue outside. The girls rushed to the door of the gym and pushed their way through. I couldn't bear to watch Lorna's body being carried back from the hockey pitch on a stretcher. I went and locked myself in one of the loos.

I could hear running feet outside the gym and men's voices. A door slammed, then another. The ambulance took off again, with its awful wail puncturing the eerie quiet of the school as it drove down the avenue and turned into the road. The head's voice sounded anxious as she shooed the onlookers back into the gym.

"Go inside, girls. Someone will be with you in five minutes."

Before long, they were back.

"Where did she go, where did she go?" I could hear them

saying. The swing doors into the cloakroom were thrust open and slapped shut. Someone whispered to the others to be quiet. Footsteps drew nearer. One by one, the doors of the cubicles were eased open. The sound of squeaking hinges grew nearer. At last, the footsteps stopped outside the loo where I was hiding.

"We know you're in there, Charlotte," said Monica, in a cold level voice. "You'll have to come out some time."

I waited, saying nothing, praying for a teacher to come and stop this madness. Suddenly the door between the cloakroom and the gym banged open once again.

"She's dead, Lorna's dead," howled Natalie's voice. "I heard Mrs O' Byrne telling the secretary."

The clamour was deafening. Fists pounded on the door.

"Get out of there, you stinking coward."

"We're coming in to get you."

A lavatory seat banged closed in the cubicle next door. There was the sound of shoes scraping against the thin wall which separated it from me. They were climbing over.

I drew back the lock and opened the door. They seemed surprised to see me, as if they had really expected to have to drag me out. I walked towards the exit, trying not to look at their spiteful faces which opened and closed like goldfish mouthing obscenities at me.

Murderer. Bastard.

I lurched through the gymnasium and came out on to the school avenue. Parked on the gravel at the front steps, I recognised Lorna's father's car with its black windows. I kept on walking, faster and faster, anxious to get away before anyone saw me. One thing was uppermost in my mind. If Lorna really was dead, nothing would stop them now.

11

DARKNESS ON DÚN LAOGHAIRE PIER

I took my time about going home, wandering aimlessly around the suburban housing estates, trying to think. My brain played back the scene on the hockey pitch again and again. There was the clash of the hockey sticks as Lorna and I hurtled forward to claim the ball, then Monica tackling from behind and the sudden searing pain as she lammed her stick against my ankles. What happened after that? I drew back my stick, lifting it a few inches off the ground, aiming at the ball. To one side, I saw the lengthening smear of brown mud as Lorna skidded, lost her balance and began to fall back in slow motion. In my mind's ear, I heard again that awful crack as my stick and her head collided. I watched the purple spreading beneath her skin and the trickle of frothy blood sliding down her chin as Monica, unseeing, seized the ball and made off with it. Her legs in retreat were huge, mottled blue and red with the cold.

Was it like that or did my temper snap? Did I see Lorna fall and seize the moment to take my revenge for all those months of cruelty? I knew which version most people in the school would go for. Why, they knew that that very morning Lorna had destroyed my best painting. No one would ever swallow a story about an accident. Especially if the victim was dead.

I stopped walking and sat down on a low wall beside a bus-stop. I was in trouble, deep trouble. My stomach was in knots as if cold bony fingers had taken hold of it, wringing it dry. I felt both hot and cold at the same time. My heart was racing. I wanted to cry, to be sick, to go to the loo, to sleep, to scrub out the whole day and start again.

A bus drew up, not the one I needed, but I pulled myself up the steps as if I was sleep-walking. On top of everything now, I was going to be very late home as I'd have to walk up from the centre of Dún Laoghaire. I wondered how I was going to face Dad and the others. Would the school already have rung home to tell them what had happened? Would anybody believe me when I said it was an accident? I doubted it. I wondered if it would be on the news that Lorna was dead. Her dad was famous enough. I was in deep, deep trouble. Maybe there was already a warrant out for my arrest.

I supposed they would send me to some sort of prison. What happened to children if they were found guilty of murder? Or was it manslaughter? Unlawful killing? Dimly remembered phrases crowded into my head from half-read newspaper articles and television broadcasts. Somewhere in the country, in some remote corner, there must be an institution for young criminals. I imagined a roomful of girls in drab grey cotton dresses, a corridor full of iron beds, high windows, straight-backed nuns wielding buckets and mops. How long would they keep me there? Would Dad come and see me? I shook my head miserably. No, he would not. He would abandon me now as surely as my mother had all those years before. I was a bad lot. I was mad. There was something wrong with me.

At every stop, the bus was picking up more and more passengers. Mothers with cranky toddlers jostled for seats among young kids in unfamiliar school uniforms, wielding violin cases and large satchels. Pensioners got on, holding everyone up as they hauled themselves up the steep steps at the door. I felt they were all staring at me, whispering to each other about me. I had started to sweat. As soon as we turned into the main street in Dún

Laoghaire, I pushed my way through the standing passengers and got off.

At the corner of Marine Road, I stopped and gasped in lungfuls of cold air. Calm down, Charlie, I was saying to myself.

"Look, there she is," came a roar a few yards away from me.

Coming out of the side entrance to the shopping centre were Natalie, Monica and Tara. Tara—that was all I needed. I hadn't seen her since the day she had left the school. I turned tail abruptly and broke into a run.

"After her!"

I dashed around the corner back on to the main street and darted in the main door of the shopping centre, hoping to get lost among the crowds there, but it was practically empty. Shop assistants were pulling down the steel grey shutters as they got ready to close up for the night. I ran past them making for the escalators in the far corner. A woman with a baby was blocking my way as she folded up the child's buggy to take it up the moving stairs. I pushed roughly past her and took the stairs at a run. At the top, I cautiously looked over the hand-rail. The girls were standing at the bottom of the escalator, unsure whether to go up or down.

"Where did she go?" I heard Tara say.

Natalie looked up. I ducked but it was too late.

"Look, there's her blazer."

I swore. How can you lose yourself in a school uniform—unless you're at school? I raced around the café to the lifts. One of the lifts was there, its doors still open. It had to be going down.

"Sorry, full up." A man held out his arm to block my way. Behind him stood a crowd of impassive faces.

"But it's important." I stuck out my foot to stop the doors from closing but the man pushed me away, bad-temperedly.

"There's no room, for Chrissake."

The doors slid shut. The lift whirred into motion. I looked around me in desperation.

"The lifts." I could hear Monica's high-pitched squeal and the scuffle of running feet. They were already rounding the corner beside the café. I took the door into the multi-storey car park.

It was dark and cold in there after the overheated air of the malls. Not many cars remained. I walked quickly past a family loading supermarket bags into the boot of their car. At the far end, I ducked down between a pillar and the car in the last parking space. A van moved slowly down the ramp from the top level, catching me in the beam of its headlamps as it swung around the corner. I caught the startled look of one of the passengers as she saw me skulking in the shadows between the pillar and the parked car.

At the other end, the doors into the car park opened and slammed shut.

"She must have come in here, Tara. Don't let her get away."

As another car came down the ramp, I ran out behind it, keeping low, and sped up to the upper level. There were more cars here but more people too. One man, fishing for his keys in his coat pocket, smiled at me as I ran past.

"Lost your mum, have you? Do you know what level the car was on?"

I ignored him and ran on towards the exit door. I came out of the car park between shopping floors on to a deserted staircase. Not very far away, I could still hear the three girls' excited squeals. Several doors banged. I stood still, listening to my breath coming in shallow gasps, and waited. Somewhere a car engine spluttered into life and began a jerky descent to street level. The lifts whirred and stopped. After a few minutes, I began to walk slowly down the stairs, trying not to make any noise.

I was just approaching the exit at the lower ground floor when I heard a short stifled snort of laughter. I froze. Silence. My imagination was working overtime. I slowly opened the door and looked out. Then they pounced. Monica seized my arm and twisted it behind my back. Tara grabbed hold of my blazer and yanked me towards her.

"Gotcha. At last."

They pushed and pulled me out to the street. Even though I was putting up a fight, dragging my feet and refusing to go with them, they just kept pulling me along like a sack of potatoes. I remember thinking how odd it was that nobody intervened. It was just like that day my mother had left me and nobody paid any attention to me. I suppose they thought we were just horsing about.

A 46A bus had just pulled up outside. I made one last effort to struggle free but all three of them held me tight. I could hear a dog barking frantically and for a moment thought it too was after me. I was cornered, like a badger in its sett and dogs baying for blood at the entrance.

Tara pushed me roughly ahead of her down Marine Road.

"Walk," she said. Wherever she had been for the last couple of months had not changed her.

"And don't even think about trying to run away. There are three of us, remember," added Monica, threateningly. To think that I had once felt sorry for her, had thought she was a victim just like me.

"Where are we going?" I half-turned my head to look at them.

"For a swim, what do you think. Just walk."

"And shut up," said Natalie, moving forward and thrusting her arm through mine so I would have no chance of escape.

The other two were just a yard or so behind me, close enough to tread on my heels. One of them prodded me in the small of my back.

They marched me down to the end of the road and on to the long stone pier which curves out about one mile into the sea, forming one arm of Dún Laoghaire harbour. It was almost deserted at that time of night. Darkness was falling and apart from a few joggers and an elderly couple walking their dogs, we saw nobody as we drew further and further away from the shore.

"What are we doing? Where are we going?" I asked.

"No questions, scumbag."

We had passed the bandstand. Two gulls, strutting by an overflowing litter bin, rose a few feet in the air as if to warn us off their patch, but flew off, screaming, when Monica stamped her feet at them.

"OK, stop here."

Tara pushed me down on to a seat by the stone wall and stood over me, flanked on either side by the other two. She was clearly in charge.

"You're dangerous, Charlie," she said. "You've really blown it this time. We'll have to punish you, you know that, don't you? We owe that to Lorna."

"But I didn't do anything. It was an accident. She slipped."

"Don't lie to us, Charlie. It'll be better for you if you don't lie." Tara's voice sounded gentle, almost reassuring. "You wanted to do it, didn't you? Tell the truth—you were planning to all along."

"I didn't, I didn't."

What were they going to do to me? My mind raced. I kept thinking of Granny Bea, waiting for me at home, getting more and more annoyed that I was late.

"Let me go," I said. "I must go home."

"We'll let you go home when you confess, Charlie. That's all you have to do." Monica thrust her face right up against mine. It occurred to me that she was by far the most dangerous, now that she was out of the cold, now that she had been accepted into the magic circle.

"It's not fair. Why do you all pick on me? I've never done anything to you."

"Now you know that isn't true, Charlie. You told lies about me," Tara's soft voice continued. "You said I was a pick-pocket. You said that I had planted that watch in your desk when you had taken it all the time."

"I didn't..."

"You didn't say I planted the watch? Or you didn't tell lies about me? she interrupted.

"Yes, no, I mean..."

"Listen to her, Monica." Tara turned away from me. "What are we going to do with her? You see, Charlie, I've tried to forgive you about the stealing and getting me thrown out of school—but how can we forgive you for hurting our friend Lorna like that. How can anyone forgive you when you've been so wicked?"

"Hurting her? You mean she's not dead?"

"You'd like that, wouldn't you?" said Natalie, smacking the side of my head. "You want her to be dead, don't you?"

"No, of course not." I looked from one to the other pleading for them to understand, to believe me. "Please tell me the truth. I thought you said at school that she was dead."

"You're the one that ought to be dead."

"You're nothing but trouble."

"Ever since you came to our school."

"Everyone hates you."

"Even your mother."

I winced with pain and put my hands to my mouth.

"You're useless," sneered Tara, her voice hard and bitter now. "Just look at you—the way you chew your nails and pull out your hair. You're just disgusting."

I stood up and angrily pushed her out of my way. They circled around me, screaming and flapping like gulls, forcing me to step back until I was just a couple of feet from the edge of the pier. I glanced over my shoulder. Behind me lay a black expanse of water, deep and cold and still. Oily slicks of spilt diesel shone in the reflected lamplight.

"Go on, Charlie, jump." It was Tara who spoke. She made it sound easy, as if it was the sensible thing to do.

"Do the decent thing," Natalie said, in a low emotionless

voice.

"Give everyone a break," added Monica.

I slowly turned my back on them and faced the sea. I took one step nearer the edge. Behind me, I could feel the three girls stiffen. I tried to think of any reason why I should not jump. Nobody wanted me. Even my dad wouldn't miss me. I'd just been a weight around his neck ever since the police in London had handed me over to him. If I was dead, he would be free at last, free to live the way he wanted. He could leave home, find a girl-friend... And I would be free too. It wouldn't take long to slip below the black surface of the water, allow myself to slide down, down, down. I moved forward and closed my eyes.

A dog began to bark. Someone shouted.

"Charlie! Charlie!"

The sound of my name was echoing on and on in my ears. I turned round slowly, dragging my eyes away from the shadowy blackness, as Casso arrived at my side. He grabbed me by the arms and pulled me towards him, back from the edge. Tara, Natalie and Monica had already bolted, running back towards Marine Road with Murphy snapping at their heels. Casso whistled for him to come back.

"It's all right, Charlie. You're safe now." He put his arm around my shoulders and led me away.

12

A LESSON ABOUT PACK ANIMALS

I was still trembling when we reached the bus stop. Casso kept his arm tightly around me as if to keep me warm but it was not the cold which was making me tremble. I had been so close to letting myself go, to sliding into that black water for ever, that I couldn't really believe what had happened. I kept running and rerunning the scene in my head, shocked that those girls had the power to drive me to such despair.

"Casso," I said, finally, when I could trust myself to speak without breaking down in tears. "I was going to jump. They were telling me to do it."

"It's all right, Charlie. You're safe now," he repeated softly, pulling me closer.

"Nobody is ever going to bully me again."

"That's the spirit, Charlie. You have to stand up to them."

"What were you doing on the pier anyway? Walking Murphy?"

"No, I was looking for you. I was upstairs on a 46A when I saw the girls dragging you out of the shopping centre. I tried to get down the stairs and get off the bus but it pulled away too fast. Murphy had seen you too and was barking his head off."

"I heard him," I said, remembering how I had heard a dog barking as we came out on to Marine Road.

"I thought I was probably over-reacting," Casso went on, "but, considering what you told me the last time, I got off at the next stop and walked back. I was about to give up when I saw you all out on the pier."

"Thanks, Casso. If you hadn't come..."

I left the rest of the sentence hanging in mid-air. I couldn't bring myself to say, "I might be dead."

Casso gave me a squeeze. "Does anybody know where you are?"

I shook my head.

"Well then, we'd better get you home. I'll come with you."

Murphy barked and looked up at me with his big mournful eyes.

"And you can come too," I said.

✳✳✳

As soon as I turned the key in the lock and opened the door, people poured into the hall. Noel, Vinnie, Dad, Granny Bea and Mrs O'Byrne from school all advanced towards me, flinging questions.

"Where have you been?"

"Are you all right?"

"Why did you run away?"

"What did those girls say to you at school?"

"Have you had anything to eat?"

The din was terrible. I was so pleased to see all their faces. I walked over to Dad and put my arms around him.

"Here, hold this, somebody," he said, passing his cigarette to Vinnie, and threw his arms around me.

"I'll put on a kettle," said Granny. "Come on, all of you, into the kitchen."

"Is she really dead?" I asked Dad. "Did I kill her?"

Dad held me out at arm's length so he could look directly at my face.

"Dead? Of course not! Why did you think that?"

I could have exploded with happiness.

"Casso," I said, "did you hear that?" I turned to the front door to tell him the good news but Casso and Murphy had already followed the others into the kitchen.

Mrs O'Byrne explained why she had come to the house. She had gone with Lorna in the ambulance and stayed with her until her parents had arrived. Lorna was badly concussed and had a gash. They were going to have to give her a few stitches and keep her under observation but things weren't as bad as they looked. She came straight from the hospital to set my mind at rest, she said, knowing I would be worried. Then she had found out I hadn't come home from school and put two and two together about the class blaming me. They had just decided to call the police and organise a search party when I showed up.

"Everybody blames me," I said.

"No, they don't. It was an accident. These things happen, at hockey, rugby, any contact sport."

"That's not what the rest of the class think."

"Listen, Charlie, I know what happened. You know what happened and Lorna, when she's better, will be able to tell her friends the truth about what happened. Don't worry about it."

Granny poured out cups of tea for everyone. Dad sat beside me, playing with my pony-tail.

"Well, it's not as simple as that," said Casso. Everybody turned to look at him.

"Who's that?" said Vinnie and Noel together.

"Casso," I said, "He saved my life."

"Oh," said Vinnie, stupidly, as if saving people's lives was something routine, that happened all the time.

"What's not as simple as that?" prompted Dad.

"They're right little bitches, if you'll excuse my language, Mrs Collins, those girls in Charlie's class. They were about to make her jump off the pier."

"What on earth are you talking about?" said Dad.

Casso told them what had happened on the pier, just as I had told him.

"You mean girl bullies?" said Vinnie, incredulously. "I didn't think such a thing existed."

Casso raised an eyebrow. "As my brother Trigger would say: if it looks like a duck and quacks like a duck, then it's a duck. But seriously, it's not the first time they've driven her mad. They pick on her and call her the Abandoned Baby. Something's got to be done about it before it goes any further."

"The Abandoned Baby?" said Dad, shocked.

"It'll never happen again," I said with conviction. "That's all finished."

Mrs O' Byrne stood up and zipped up her jacket. "You're telling me it'll never happen again. I'll see to that."

She gave me a kiss on her way out. I had never been kissed by a teacher before. It felt very funny. Then Casso got up to go.

"You know what you have to do now, Charlie?" he said. "You have to go back to that school tomorrow and face up to those girls." Then he kissed me lightly on the cheek. I had never been kissed by a boy before and that felt, well, even funnier.

Later on, after I had eaten my supper and was in my room, Dad knocked at the door. I was standing at the dressing-table, doing my hair. He took the brush out of my hand and began to brush my hair, fanning it out over my shoulders. All the time he talked to my reflection in the glass.

"You know I love you, Charlie. Sometimes I'm not good at showing it but you're the best thing that ever happened to me. I'd swing for anyone that hurt you." As he said that, he yanked my hair down with the brush.

"Hey," I yelled, "that hurt."

Our reflections smiled at one another.

"Would you really have thrown yourself in the sea, Charlie?" he asked.

"Yes, I think I might have. I was so scared and hurt inside. I didn't know what else I could do. They were always picking on me, making me feel useless and hateful. I felt completely desperate, as if I'd never get away from them. And I thought I was in dead trouble because of Lorna. I thought I might be sent away to prison."

"Poor Charlie. And do they really call you the Abandoned Baby?"

I nodded.

Dad put the hairbrush on the dressing-table and sat down on the side of the bed.

"I know it's hard for you to believe this now but your mother probably thought she was doing the best thing for you."

"How do you mean?" I asked, frowning.

"She knew she couldn't look after you, that it wasn't fair bringing you up in squats, living rough. It wasn't that she didn't love you. She did love you—that's why she gave you back to me."

Tears welled up in my eyes. I couldn't speak. In the end Dad broke the silence.

"Have you ever seen a group of cats hunting together?" he said.

I shook my head, wondering what he was going to say next.

"That's because they don't. Cats hunt creatures that are smaller than themselves, mice or birds, so they hunt alone. Animals that hunt prey that are bigger than themselves need to co-operate, they need to hunt in a pack, like wolves chasing reindeer."

"Why are you telling me this, Dad?"

"Because the girls in your class have been bullying you in a gang—that means you must be bigger than them. Remember that."

He kissed the top of my head and walked over to the door.

"One more thing, Charlie, that boy Casso—is he your boyfriend?"

"Da-ad," I said, turning a brilliant shade of red.

"Just asking. He's a good guy." He stopped again, half-in and half-out of the room. "Maybe I got it wrong when I said he came from a rough lot. I seem to have got a lot of things wrong recently."

When he had gone, I looked at my face in the mirror. My face looked back at me and smiled.

"Look at me," I said, "I'm alive. I'm strong. I'm bigger than they are." And I leaned over and gave myself a kiss.

Before I got into bed, I did one last thing. I took out the photo of my mother, of Lisa, from where I had hidden it behind the bookcase and stuck it in a corner of the mirror. Everybody would see her now.

"Look here," I said to the face which looked so like my own. "Maybe you weren't so wicked after all but, sometimes, people are entitled to make a fuss."

13

MARBLE ARCH REMEMBERED

B ut I could not sleep. Every time I began to drift off, the darkness closed in around me, reminding me of the black oily waters off the pier. I felt myself sinking, being slowly drawn down into a watery black hole. I struggled to wake up, forcing myself to keep my eyes open, pushing the nightmare away. My skin had become wet and clammy and I felt smothered by the weight of the duvet. I kicked it down to my feet and took long deep breaths to try and relax. For a long time I lay listening to the sounds of the old house creaking and settling for the night. The water tank gurgled and growled, the staircase groaned. In a nearby room, low rhythmic snores started up.

This is my home, I thought. There is nothing to be frightened of here but something was bothering me, making sleep impossible—something my dad had said earlier.

"It wasn't that she didn't love you. She did love you—that's why she gave you back to me."

Did that make sense, I wondered. Could such a cruel thing be done for love? And then it all began to come back to me.

The city never sleeps, said Lisa. She held my hand tightly in hers and pulled me across the vast city square, weaving in and out between the lanes of cars which bore down on us, horns blaring. Lisa laughed at them. In the harsh yellow light of the street lamps, her face glowed, excited, carefree. Rows of buses were lined up along one side, long single-decker coaches, not the usual red double-deckers which we sometimes took, but we did not join a queue. Instead we plunged down a staircase which led underground, into a maze of dimly lit tunnels. We passed dark bulky shapes, bodies already sleeping under makeshift piles of blankets and clothes, bin-liners and newspapers. It was like another city down there, crowded with bodies almost touching one another, but each in its own carefully guarded space. Lisa unfolded a large square of cardboard in an empty space beneath a wall light and laid out two sleeping bags upon it.

"I don't want to sleep here, Mummy. I'm cold."

"Just for one night, Charlie," she repeated, laying her fingers on my lips so that I wouldn't talk any more. "I'll be here beside you."

I sat down on the sleeping bag closest to the wall. Lisa took off my shoes and pushed them down into the bottom corner.

"Here, don't take off your clothes," she said, "button up your coat again. It's just for one night, pet."

She tucked me into the bag and sat down beside me. I could hear her light up a cigarette and smelled the acrid smoke drift back towards me. It mingled with the stench of the damp running down the walls of the tunnel and the urine-reeking floor. My stomach heaved but I burrowed down deeper into the nylon bag, willing myself not to be sick.

Men were coughing, hacking away in the darkness. Others snored, long even snores which occasionally broke their rhythm and restarted with a violent vibrating growl as the sleeper fought for breath. Shadows fell across where I lay as figures moved among the sleeping bodies, lurching against the walls, crying out in drunken or drugged terrors. Now and then, I heard the patter of tiny scampering feet and Lisa's sharp intake of breath as the rats ran past her. I pressed myself against her back, looking for comfort. I could feel her tense and watchful beside me, lighting and re-lighting her cigarettes, trying to keep awake. She hummed to herself, songs with sad words I could not understand.

Once I woke to a dreadful crash. Splintered glass showered over us and a crazy woman in a fur hat staggered towards us.

"Turn off the bloody light," she screamed, "it's time you all turned off the bloody light."

She had thrown a bottle against the wall light.

Lisa pushed my head under the sleeping bag. I could feel her fingers moving over me, picking up the shards of glass which covered my sleeping bag. My nostrils filled with the smell of cider from the broken bottle. Lisa's sniffs told me she was crying, crying quietly so as not to frighten me.

Later I woke again. Lisa was shouting.

"Keep your hands off me, you dirty—let go of me."

She was standing up, hitting out at someone, her arms flailing.

Other voices shouted back.

"Shut up, will you?"

"Stop the bloody racket, woman. Some of us are trying to sleep."

A man stumbled unsteadily down the passageway towards the staircase. I let myself drift back to sleep. Some time later, Lisa was bending over me, gently shaking my shoulder.

"Come on, Charlie. Time to get up." She touched my face with stiff, cold fingers. I think I started to cry.

"Come on, Charlie, please don't make a fuss, not now. I've got to get you of here."

We came out of the tunnel and walked across to the underground station. It was raining lightly but the air seemed so sweet and fresh after the stench of the underpass. Lisa moved quickly. We must be going somewhere, I thought. We stood, silently, hand in hand, waiting for the tube to arrive. I had a chocolate bar in my other hand. She must have bought it from the machine in the station.

Then these memories flowed into the torrent of memories of

that far-off Christmas Eve. They flooded over me, the memories I had kept locked away all those years, never letting on to Dad how much I knew. I began to understand why my mother had decided to leave me.

I remembered the roar of the train as it came out of the tunnel and rattled to a stop at the platform. We passed a man playing a guitar and climbed the long wooden moving stairs up to the main concourse. She set me down on a little step outside a shop. I could see her thin, white, tired face leaning over me and saying, wait here a minute, Charlie, I have to make a call. She stroked my face and leant down to whisper to me, "come on, Charlie, help Mummy, don't make a fuss." As she turned to go, she pushed a piece of paper deep into the pocket of my coat. Look after that for me, she said, don't lose it.

So I waited quietly, sitting on the little step, breathing in the sweet fruity smells of Body Shop soaps, waiting for my mother to come back. Legs rushed past me; for a time, men in uniforms came and played carols, their music sheets clipped on to little stands at the ends of their instruments. Crackly voices called out the names of trains. A long time passed. Then the policeman went down on his hunkers to talk to me and I wet my pants. The waiting was almost over.

I threw the duvet off and got out of bed. Through the slats of the blinds, I could see a crack of sky. A weak sun was breaking through the clouds, suffusing the room with a pink light. I picked up the photograph from the dressing table and took it over to the window. In it, Lisa's face was turned upwards towards my dad's.

I went in to my father's bedroom. It was time to talk.

Dad stirred the moment I opened his door. He lifted his head and squinted at me.

"What's the matter, Charlie? Is there something wrong?"

"I remember everything, Dad, about the day Lisa left me in Victoria, and the night before. I thought you ought to know."

He stretched out a hand towards his wrist-watch lying on the bedside table.

"What time is it? Six o'clock already?" He sat up in bed and ran his fingers through his hair.

"Why did you never talk about it?"

"I hoped you'd forgotten, that your mind would close it all out. I thought forgetting was all for the best."

"It only made me feel guilty, as if it was a bad secret I must never tell anyone. I believed it was probably my own fault," I said fiercely. "I thought I must have been a bad person."

Dad looked up at me sharply. "Okay, Charlie, let's talk. Go and put on a kettle. I'll be right down. Don't wake the rest of the house."

As we sipped tea, I told him how, the night before she abandoned me, Lisa and I had slept in the underpass in London.

"I think we must have done it lots of times."

"We guessed you must have been living rough. After the first shock and the anger, we tried to imagine why she had done it. She must have realised she couldn't cope, that you wouldn't have survived on the streets. You were very underweight when we found you, and pretty dirty too." He smiled at me over his cup. "A real little waif."

"Did she not get in touch with you afterwards? Did you not look for her?"

"Of course we looked for her—everyone did, us, the police, the Salvation Army, the press. The story was in all the papers, here and in England. She never came forward. It was as if she had just disappeared off the face of the earth. Apparently people do it all the time."

"But you've seen her, haven't you, Dad? Tell me the truth. I saw her name on the yellow pad beside the phone. I heard you talking to her once when I came in from school."

Dad stared at me with a pained, shocked expression, as if I had struck him. Unshaven and unwashed in the early morning light, he looked much older.

"No, Charlie," he answered, "but I did try to find out what had become of her when you started to ask questions. I could see you needed to know more than I could tell you. I rang her mother."

I cut him off abruptly. "Her mother lives here? You know her? Does she know me?"

"She lives in the flats, near your friend Casso. I suppose that's the real reason I didn't want you going around there though it wouldn't have mattered anyway. She couldn't tell me anything."

"Did you believe her?"

Dad nodded his head slowly. "Yes, I did. Lisa has never once come back to Ireland or phoned or sent a Christmas card, not since she went to London to have you. She never had any time for her family, hated family life. That's why she wouldn't even tell them she had a baby. I expect that's the reason she walked out on me too."

"So what do you think has happened to her?" I took a deep breath. "Do you think she might be dead?"

Dad looked at me closely as if calculating what I could take. "Maybe, Charlie," he replied, at last. "If she stayed on the streets, if she kept taking drugs, she could be. But maybe not. Maybe she has built a new life for herself. Let's believe she's happy somewhere."

"I don't feel so bad about her any more," I said. "Perhaps she was the victim of the whole story, not me. She did what she did to help me, not to hurt me."

"Yes," agreed Dad. "It was a desperate way to show her love for you but I agree that is probably why she did it."

85

14

BUILDING FOUNDATIONS

A couple of hours later I set off for school. Dad had tried to persuade me to take the day off and go back to bed but that would only have postponed the evil moment when I had to face up to the bullies as Casso had told me to do. The problem was I didn't have a clue what I was going to do. I ran through all sorts of little scenes in my head, the way you do, with everybody being dead sensible and logical and me getting my own way in the end. "Listen, Tara and Monica and Lorna and Natalie, this bullying will have to end."

"Okay, Charlie, you're right."

No, that wouldn't work.

Why had they picked on me to bully anyway? I reckoned you're only bullied if you are different in some way—weaker, or smaller, or posher, or fatter or cleverer or spottier than everybody else. Or the only black person in a white school or really thick. What was I? I was the Abandoned Baby. And that made me weak. Well, I was going to have to be strong from now on.

I didn't feel very strong, though, as I walked through the gates. I was half hoping that Natalie and Monica would be absent and praying that the word was out that Lorna was going to be all right so I didn't have the whole class hissing 'murderer' at me again. More than anything, I hoped that I would have the guts to see the day through to the end.

Slam. My head collided with the cloakroom wall with an ominous crack. For an instant I saw stars. Someone grabbed my arms fiercely and twisted them behind my back.

"One word about last night and you're dead meat," said Monica.

"Too late," I said, as calmly as I could, as the pain shot up my arm. "I've already told."

"Come off it, Charlie," she sneered. "Who did you tell—your stupid boy-friend and his mangy dog?" She tightened her grip on my arm and wrenched it higher.

"Monica," I said, twisting my head around so that I could look her pitted pizza face in the eye, "they're just using you. If I were you, I wouldn't trust them. They'll drop you again, you wait and see."

Monica's grip on my arm relaxed. She flung it away from her and shuffled off to the door.

"Piss off, Charlie," she shouted. "Nobody is using me."

Good, I thought to myself afterwards, not a bad start.

At lunch time the corridors were already deserted as I made my way back towards my form-room. As I turned into the passage past the staff-room, I heard raised voices as if someone was having an argument. The words "Dún Laoghaire pier" stopped me in my tracks. I moved closer to the door to hear what was going on.

"... as I understand it, the child was going to kill herself." It was Mrs O' Byrne, the gym teacher.

There was a familiar snort of derision. That had to be Mrs Armstrong.

"Nonsense, Joan. The girl has always been difficult, prone to exaggeration, unstable, if you ask me."

"She has made it hard for people to like her," agreed the head. "She doesn't join in things, keeps herself far too much to herself..."

"I think we need to face the fact that she was deliberately

excluded," said Mrs O'Byrne. "Lorna Higgins is a very forceful character. She has all the rest of them under her thumb."

"Fiddlesticks. Lorna's a born leader, a very attractive girl. I can't see her in the role of bully at all. If you ask me, this whole business is just Charlotte's imagination."

"Quite," agreed the head. "She was worried about the incident on the hockey pitch and her imagination ran away with her."

As Mrs O'Byrne started to speak, the head cut her off abruptly. "I know you're concerned, Joan, but just at the moment I'm much more worried about Lorna's father. He's threatening to sue us. A scandal is the last thing we want on our hands. The building programme for the science block is already months behind schedule. If the school's reputation suffers, the fund-raising will dry up."

"But it was an accident. Charlotte didn't attack Lorna deliberately."

"Well, you certainly seem to think so." There was no mistaking from the tone of her voice that Mrs Armstrong did not think so.

"And one other thing, while we're all here. I'm re-considering Tara's expulsion. Apparently she hasn't settled in at all well at her new school. I think we may have acted too hastily."

Someone stood up and sighed. I could hear a chair being scraped back on the wooden floor.

"Of course I haven't made my decision. I'm interviewing her and her parents later on today."

There was more movement inside the staff-room. Other chairs were pulled back and footsteps moved towards the door.

"All I'm saying is we have to be even-handed," said the head's voice again. "Why don't we all keep a close eye on the situation and talk about it again after the Easter holidays?"

"Fine," said Armstrong, "but, let's face it, this isn't some rough inner-city school. You don't find bullying in a girls' school like this."

You're so blind, I thought. You only see what you want to see.

Nothing else exists. But I didn't want adults solving my problems, anyway. Tackling the bullies was something I had to do by myself. I hurried away, doubling back the way I had come.

Several times during the next few hours I was aware of Natalie and Monica watching me. They sat close together, their heads almost touching, whispering conspiratorially. Even when they were finally separated during maths, they kept up an unending exchange of notes. But if they were up to something, they didn't have the chance to carry it out. The final bell rang. Everyone was in a rush to leave for it was the last day of term before the Easter holidays. I hung back until most of the other girls had gone, then legged it towards the short-cut through the building site.

It was oddly quiet even though it was still early in the afternoon. Maybe the heavy rain had forced the men to stop work or perhaps they had already knocked off for their Easter break. I boldly walked past the DANGER KEEP OUT sign, stooped down behind the site manager's hut and listened. Nothing but the clatter of magpies in the trees beyond and the distant rumble of traffic from the main road. And yet I knew I was not alone: someone was there, stalking me. They hadn't given up at all. They were just up to their usual tricks, waiting for me to leave the school premises. I remembered what my dad had told me the night before—animals who hunt together stalk a bigger prey. Right, I told myself, you are bigger than they are. And you know they're after you.

The high yellow crane loomed over the site, its massive base standing in the deep rectangular hole which had been cleared for the foundations of the classrooms. The panels which surrounded the trench had been covered in graffiti which the builders had half-heartedly tried to paint out with swirling blocks of black colour, probably at the head's instructions. I darted out from behind the shelter of the hut and circled round behind a pile of wooden pallets to the towering mound of soil that had been dumped to one side. It was no longer strewn with the pretty pink blossom of the cherry trees as it had been when I did the painting. In the rain, the black clay looked thick and slippery, with water running off it and forming a quagmire of mud all around. A mechanical digger lay abandoned and lopsided near the foot of the mound, one of its large muddy wheels hanging in mid-air.

"Charlie!"

I swung around just as a stone whizzed over my head and landed with a splash in a puddle at my feet. I took cover behind the digger and scanned the site. Nothing moved. The rain was pelting down, bouncing off the unfinished mud track through the site. I was getting soaked. I turned up the collar of my blazer and ran out in the direction of the gaping hole in the fence which gave on to the lane down to the railway station.

Another stone whizzed over my head. And another. The next one just brushed my cheek.

Something in me exploded then. This thing had to be settled before another term started, another term of abuse and hatred. I turned around and roared at the top of my voice.

"Come out and fight then, if you dare. I'm not afraid of you." I stooped down and picked up a piece of broken brick.

There was no reply but behind the pile of wooden pallets I sensed something move, imagined I saw a flash of blue.

I raised the brick, ready to lob it for all it was worth as soon as they attacked again.

A figure appeared from behind the pallets. Natalie began to climb up into the cab of the digger. It seemed to totter as she pulled herself into the seat. There was a low rumble. A trickle of loose stones bounced down the heap of earth. A flock of birds rose out of the trees and flew off squawking noisily. Then there was a long wet slithering noise which grew in momentum as the soil shifted. There was a loud thump as it fell against the perimeter fence. As I watched, open-mouthed with horror, the fence shuddered violently. For an instant it grew still again.

Then, suddenly there came a wrenching, tearing noise as the weight of the sliding earth bombarded it. The fence collapsed backwards in slow motion, toppling over into the foundations, carrying with it an avalanche of thick slimy black soil. A thick cloud of dust rose up and fell slowly back to earth. An eerie hush descended over the site.

I ran forwards, too shocked to call out.

Natalie was the first person I saw. She was lying on the ground where she had been thrown when the digger fell over but as I came closer she moved and pulled herself to her feet.

"Are you all right?" I asked. Her face, under the smears of mud, was drained of all colour. She was rubbing her hands up and down her legs and arms as if astonished to find herself still in one piece. When I spoke to her again, she pulled her coat closely around her and stared all about, like a frightened colt ready to bolt.

"Where are the others?" I said, sternly. "Who was with you?"

"Natalie! Is that you, Natalie? Help!" A strangled cry came from below where the fence had collapsed. I moved gingerly towards it, glancing uncertainly over my shoulder at what remained of the pile of soil, and peered down into the foundations. The digger lay on its side, its back wheels suspended over the edge. Beneath it, the soft sagging face of Monica stared up at me. She was half buried in the thick wet muck.

"Are you hurt?" I called.

"I'm stuck," she said, her face crumpling. "Please don't go away, Charlie." Awful ugly sounds tore from her throat. Her round shoulders rose and fell as her sobs grew louder.

I turned back towards Natalie.

"We'll have to get her out together."

"No," said Natalie, backing away. "She can do it herself. I've got to go."

"No," I shouted back, seizing her arm. "You have to help. She's your friend." I lowered my voice so Monica would not hear. "The digger could fall in on top of her if more of that soil shifts."

"We'll never budge her. She's too fat and heavy for us to get her out. Go back to the school and call the fire brigade if you want."

"So you'd just abandon her, would you?"

That word. Abandon. Natalie flinched and turned her eyes away from me.

"Why should you care anyway?" she muttered.

"Just do it, Natalie."

I walked back to the edge and looked down on Monica.

"Can't you try and wriggle out at all?"

She shook her head, hopelessly, and started to cry again. "I think I've hurt my leg. Anyway I'm stuck. There's nothing to hold on to."

"All right, hang on, Monica," I said, "we're going to get you out."

"How can we?" said Natalie. "We haven't got a rope or anything."

"We'll have to do something else then," I said, sharply.

I lay down on the ground and edged forward until I was half hanging into the hole. Monica was way beyond my reach. I looked back over my shoulder. Natalie was standing a few yards away, wiping mud off her coat.

"Grab my legs, Natalie," I said.

She came forward unenthusiastically and limply held on to my ankles.

"Tightly," I said. "You won't catch any germs."

I lowered myself further over the edge, letting Natalie take my weight, but I could see this would never work. Unless Monica got herself out of the mud and stood up, I'd never reach her.

"I can't do it, Charlie. It's no use. Oh God, I'm going to die," she wailed.

Behind me, Natalie's nails pressed into my flesh as she

struggled to hang on to me.

"Charlie, my hands are too wet. I can't hold on any more. I'm going to drop you." Natalie's voice rose in panic.

"Okay, pull me back."

The digger beside us groaned menacingly and shifted slightly. One of its back wheels trembled.

I lay panting on the ground, my head spinning from hanging upside down.

"We'll have to jump in and dig her out," I said. "That digger could topple over any time."

"Then we'll all be stranded down there. How will we get back up?"

We turned and looked around the site. There was nothing useful lying around, no ladders, no tools.

"I know," said Natalie. "We'll use those pallets to make a platform."

Together, we dragged the heavy pallets over to the side of the foundations where the fence had given way. Monica had stopped crying and was slumped over on the muddy earth below us. We looked at her uneasily. "Now what?" I said.

"I'll jump down first," she replied. "I'm taller than you. Then you lower the pallets to me."

We worked as fast as we could, hoisting the heavy pieces of wood until we had about half a dozen of them laid one on top of the other in an unsteady pile on the muddy earth. Then I dropped down on top of them and jumped down beside Natalie.

Monica was in deep shock. Her face and arms had gone completely white. I touched her forehead. It was icy cold.

"Come on," I said, "there's no time to lose."

We scrabbled at the wet caked earth, with our bare hands, pushing it away from Monica's limp body. Then, catching her under her arms, we tried to prise her free. Overhead loomed the enormous arm of the crane and the teetering shadow of the digger. My hands and Natalie's moved swiftly in unison as if they were joined to the same body, working to the commands of a single brain.

I found myself repeating over and over to myself the horrible litany of names they had called me: Snotty Lottie, Murderer, Apple Charlotte, the Bastard, the Abandoned Baby, Grass, Boffin, and the number of times they had run away from me, shouting "Charlotte's germs" if I touched them or anything that belonged to them. They had made me hate myself, had driven me to such despair I wanted to kill myself. They had almost succeeded. I looked at Natalie's face. She lowered her eyes.

Finally, with one last monstrous tug, we pulled Monica free from the sticky black mud. Her legs, black and plastered with dirt, were badly cut. Blood oozed from behind her knees. As soon as she saw it, she groaned and passed out.

We hauled her to our makeshift platform and hoisted her up on to it. Doubling under her weight, we lifted her up on to level ground.

"Come on, Monica," said Natalie, "it's not that bad. Can't you walk?"

Monica gave a little groan.

"What'll we do now?" I said.

"Play ambulance men, I suppose," answered Natalie.

We got her to lie down on another pallet. Then, one at each end, we staggered across the building site back to the now deserted school grounds. As we emerged from behind the Danger, Keep Out sign, the principal came walking down the avenue with Tara and her father. We set our makeshift stretcher and Monica down on the ground. The head's mouth opened and snapped shut. Natalie and I looked at one another and at Monica lying groaning and bleeding on the wooden pallet and tried not to laugh. Mucky wasn't the word.

"Sorry, Charlie," said Natalie.

"Yeah, sorry Charlie," wheezed Monica, pulling herself to her feet and yanking her muddy skirt over her knees as the head bore down on us.

On the way home, I went in to a shop, even though I looked such a state, and picked up a lottery ticket for that night's mid-week draw. I was breaking the routine—it wasn't Saturday and it wasn't my job to pick up the cards but I was feeling lucky. Granny would lend me my pocket money early, if I asked her nicely, so I could go back to the shop to put in my entry in time. And, I decided, I would change my numbers. Nothing in my life was going to be the same again.

After the eight o'clock news on television that night, I waited to hear the results of the draw. Nobody else was interested. Granny didn't gamble and Dad hadn't entered.

On the screen, the balls floated in a large round drum.

"Please, please, please, let me win," I wished.

Number four. My age when I was left in London, no, be positive—my age when I came to Dublin. Got it.

Number fourteen. My age now. Got it. Steady on, Charlie, keep a grip.

Number thirty-three. No. Never mind.

Number twenty-two. Oh well, it's only a game.

Number thirty-one. Today's date. Yes, yes, yes. I've got three numbers.

And number seven. The number of pallets we used. Excellent. I've won four numbers. I've won a prize.

I ran out into the hall, screaming, hysterical.

"I've won the lottery, come quick, everybody. I've won the lottery."

"You've all the numbers?" Dad came flying down the stairs, taking them three at a time.

"Well, just four. But I've won something."

Dad's excited face grew a little less excited.

"Well done, Charlie. That'll be about twenty pounds, I reckon, enough to dry-clean your uniform."

"Da-ad!"

He grinned. "Keep your hair on, just a joke."

"When can I get my winnings?" I flung my arms around him.

"Calm down. I'll pick it up tomorrow at the shop, or Blackrock post office, after work. You won't be able to get it yourself—kids aren't supposed to gamble. I'll have to sign the back of the ticket."

Tomorrow. I wanted it right now, just to finish off the day on a high note.

Dad saw my disappointed face.

"Or we could go now to the shop, if you like. It stays open until half-past nine. On one condition—you buy me a cream egg."

Bliss.

15

CHARLIE'S FINAL TASK

I woke to hear the first lawn-mower of the season start up noisily in a neighbour's garden. The smell of toast drifted upstairs and under my bedroom door, teasing me to get up and join the others for breakfast, but I resisted and allowed myself another five minutes snuggled deep under the duvet. The sun was shining through the window blinds, casting a grid of patterned light and shadow on the wall opposite me and on the dressing-table where my lottery winnings lay—two tenners, a fiver and a handful of change. £28. What was I going to do with it? None of the big projects for sure. The luxury house for Granny was out, as was the farm for Noel, the cable cars up Errigal for Dad, the flights on Concorde and the cruise down the Nile. Even a pair of state-of-the-art trainers was still beyond my reach. I didn't care. In fact, twenty-eight pounds seemed perfect, an ideal amount of money to have to spend, and the Easter holidays to spend it in.

I let my eyes wander around the room, over my old teddy, Gary Gatwick, sitting precariously on the narrow window-sill, in danger of toppling off as usual if anyone banged the front door too hard. Memories of how I came to have old Gary led me to the photo of Lisa and my dad tucked under a corner of the dressing-table mirror. I wasn't abandoned that day, I thought, I was found. My Dad found me. And I found him and Granny, and

Uncle Noel and Vinnie and the rest of them. I didn't have a bad parent, who didn't love me. I had a very good parent who rescued me. I was no victim. Nobody would bully me again. I was really lucky—look, I had even won the lottery.

There was one other thing I knew I had to do, something that could be put off no longer. After breakfast, I took the bus to Dún Laoghaire. The sun had brought everyone out so the town was thronged with smiling people wearing tee-shirts and summer dresses, the way people do when they think the winter has finally ended, even though it wasn't all that warm. Small children ambled along eating ice-cream cones, and a toddler in a sun-hat was teetering along on tiptoes pushing her own buggy along the promenade. A heat haze hung over the bay, blurring the edges of the pier and softening the bright colours of the sailing boats moored in the harbour so that it seemed as if we were all living in a water-colour.

I bought a bunch of sweet-smelling yellow freesia in the centre, then thought that looked too mean so went back and bought another.

The man at the reception desk told me the room number. I went up in the lift with two nuns and a priest, feeling ridiculous.

I knocked softly at the door, a little half-heartedly, I admit, as if a part of me still hoped I didn't have to do this, that I would have an excuse to go away again if no one answered. A woman's voice told me to come in.

Lorna was lying on her side facing the open window but did not turn when the door opened. Her mother, pinning get-well cards to the wall opposite the bed, looked startled, almost frightened when she saw me. The room smelled of fruit and flowers and disinfectant.

I waved the flowers at her, feeling very foolish.

"I just came to see how Lorna was and to give her these. I'll leave them if she's sleeping." I laid the freesia at the foot of the bed and started to back towards the door.

"Is that Charlie?" Lorna turned her head slowly as if it still pained her to move and sat up. She looked thin and deflated, as if life had been squeezed out of her. One side of her head had been partly shaved. A neat line of stitches ran behind her ear like a miniature railway track. Our eyes met. All the rage and pain that she had caused me came welling up in me. The names. The mean destructive acts of bullying. Most of all, the exclusion zone she and her friends had built around me. Twice I might have been killed because of her.

Go home, Charlie, I said to myself. You shouldn't have come.

I was about to turn and leave the room when Lorna held out her arms. For an instant I thought she was holding up her arms to shield herself as if I might do her harm and shook my head.

"I'm sorry, Charlie."

I stumbled across the room the short distance to her bed and hugged her. I could feel her wet face against mine.

"I'm sorry too," I whispered, hoarsely.

"No, Charlie, don't say that. This," she gingerly felt her shaven head and smiled ruefully, "this wasn't your fault. I'm the one who's sorry. We were so cruel. I heard what they did to you afterwards."

Behind us I heard the click of the door closing as Lorna's mother let herself out.

"Are you going to be all right?" I asked. My eyes flickered up to her head and the alarming scar behind her ear.

"Yes," said Lorna. "Are you?"

"Yes," I nodded. "I'm going to be fine."

We looked down on the harbour, on the silvery pool of water and the bobbing sailing-boats held in the embrace of the east and west piers. From where we were sitting in the hospital room high above everyone, the strolling figures looked tiny and unreal. I was thinking how beautiful it looked now, shimmering in the soft light of the afternoon sun, a far cry from the night I had almost thrown myself off the edge into the deep dark water.

And suddenly the pain and the misery of the last year were all behind me. I felt like singing. Look at me, I wanted to shout, I'm strong. And I'll make a fuss if I want to.

Look for other BEACON BOOKS
published by Poolbeg

*"Literary books for discriminating
young adult readers"*

❧

Song of the River by Soinbhe Lally

Charlie's Story by Maeve Friel

Circling the Triangle by Margrit Cruickshank

The Homesick Garden by Kate Cruise O'Brien

When Stars Stop Spinning by Jane Mitchell

Shadow Boxer by Chris Lynch

❧

BEACON BOOKS